THE
VOICE
OF THE DOLPHINS

and Other Stories

by Leo Szilard

SIMON AND SCHUSTER • NEW YORK • 1961

"REPORT ON 'GRAND CENTRAL TERMINAL,'" REPRINTED FROM "THE UNI-
VERSITY OF CHICAGO MAGAZINE," JUNE 1952. "MY TRIAL AS A WAR
CRIMINAL," REPRINTED FROM "THE UNIVERSITY OF CHICAGO LAW RE-
VIEW," VOL. 17, NO. 1, AUTUMN, 1949.

"NIGHTMARE FOR FUTURE REFERENCE" FROM "SELECTED WORKS OF
STEPHEN VINCENT BENÉT," COPYRIGHT © 1938 BY STEPHEN VINCENT
BENÉT. REPRINTED BY PERMISSION OF HOLT, RINEHART & WINSTON, INC.

Contents

Nightmare for Future Reference

BY STEPHEN VINCENT BENÉT

Nightmare for Future Reference

BY STEPHEN VINCENT BENÉT

That was the second year of the Third World War,
The one between Us and Them.
                                        Well, we've gotten used.
We don't talk much about it, queerly enough.
There was all sorts of talk the first years after the Peace,
A million theories, a million wild suppositions,
A million hopeful explanations and plans,
But we don't talk about it now. We don't even ask.
We might do the wrong thing. I don't guess you'd understand
    that.
But you're eighteen now. You can take it. You'd better know.

You see, you were born just before the war broke out.
Who started it? Oh, they said it was Us or Them

and it looked like it at the time. You don't know what that's like.
But anyhow, it started and there it was,
Just a little worse, of course, than the one before,
But mankind was used to that. We didn't take notice.
They bombed our capital and we bombed theirs.
You've been to the Broken Towns? Yes, they take you there.
They show you the look of the tormented earth.
But they can't show the smell or the gas or the death
Or how it felt to be there, and a part of it.
But we didn't know. I swear that we didn't know.

I remember the first faint hint there was something wrong,
Something beyond all wars and bigger and strange,
Something you couldn't explain.
                              I was back on leave—
Strange, as you felt on leave, as you always felt—
But I went to see the Chief at the hospital,
And there he was, in the same old laboratory,
A little older, with some white in his hair,
But the same eyes that went through you and the same tongue.
They hadn't been able to touch him—not the bombs
Nor the ruin of his life's work nor anything.
He blinked at me from behind his spectacles
And said, "Huh. It's you. They won't let me have guinea pigs
Except for the war work, but I steal a few.
And they've made me a colonel—expect me to salute.
Damn fools. A damn-fool business. I don't know how.
Have you heard what Erickson's done with the ductless glands?
The journals are four months late. Sit down and smoke."
And I did and it was like home.
                              He was a great man.
You might remember that—and I'd worked with him.
Well, finally he said to me, "How's your boy?"

"Oh—healthy," I said. "We're lucky."
                                    "Yes," he said,
And a frown went over his face. "He might even grow up,

Though the intervals between wars are getting shorter.
I wonder if it wouldn't simplify things
To declare mankind in a permanent state of siege.
It might knock some sense in their heads."
                                        "You're cheerful," I said.
"Oh, I'm always cheerful," he said. "Seen these, by the way?"
He tapped some charts on a table.
                              "Seen what?" I said.
"Oh," he said, with that devilish, sidelong grin of his,
"Just the normal city statistics—death and birth.
You're a soldier now. You wouldn't be interested.
But the birth rate's dropping."
                              "Well, really, sir," I said,
"We know that it's always dropped, in every war."

"Not like this," he said. "I can show you the curve.
It looks like the side of a mountain, going down.
And faster, the last three months—yes, a good deal faster.
I showed it to Lobenheim and he was puzzled.
It makes a neat problem—yes?" He looked at me.

"They'd better make peace," he said. "They'd better make
      peace."

"Well, sir," I said, "if we break through, in the spring . . ."

"Break through?" he said. "What's that? They'd better make
      peace.
The stars may be tired of us. No, I'm not a mystic.
I leave that to the big scientists in bad novels.
But I never saw such a queer maternity curve.
I wish I could get to Ehrens, on their side.
He'd tell me the truth. But the fools won't let me do it."

His eyes looked tired as he stared at the careful charts.
"Suppose there are no more babies?" he said. "What then?

13

It's one way of solving the problem."
                                        "But, sir—" I said.
"But, sir!" he said. "Will you tell me, please, what is life?
Why it's given, why it's taken away?
Oh, I know—we make a jelly inside a test tube,
We keep a cock's heart living inside a jar.
We know a great many things, and what do we know?
We think we know what finished the dinosaurs,
But do we? Maybe they were given a chance
And then it was taken back. There are other beasts
That only kill for their food. No, I'm not a mystic,
But there's a certain pattern in nature, you know,
And we're upsetting it daily. Eat and mate
And go back to the earth after that, and that's all right.
But now we're blasting and sickening earth itself.
She's been very patient with us. I wonder how long."

Well, I thought the Chief had gone crazy, just at first,
And then I remembered the look of no man's land,
That bitter landscape, pockmarked like the moon,
Lifeless as the moon's face and horrible,
The thing we'd made with the guns.
                                        If it were earth,
It looked as though it hated.
                                "Well?" I said,
And my voice was a little thin. He looked hard at me.
"Oh—ask the women," he grunted. "Don't ask me.
Ask them what they think about it."
                                        I didn't ask them,
Not even your mother—she was strange, those days—
But, two weeks later, I was back in the lines
And somebody sent me a paper—
Encouragement for the troops and all of that—
All about the fall of Their birth rate on Their side.

I guess you know now. There was still a day when we fought,

14

And the next day the women knew. I don't know how they knew,
But they smashed every government in the world
Like a heap of broken china, within two days,
And we'd stopped firing by then. And we looked at each other.

We didn't talk much, those first weeks. You couldn't talk.
We started in rebuilding and that was all,
And at first nobody would even touch the guns,
Not even to melt them up. They just stood there, silent,
Pointing the way they had and nobody there.
And there was a kind of madness in the air,
A quiet, bewildered madness, strange and shy.
You'd pass a man who was muttering to himself
And you'd know what he was muttering, and why.
I remember coming home and your mother there.
She looked at me, at first didn't speak at all,
And then she said, "Burn those clothes. Take them off and burn
    them
Or I'll never touch you or speak to you again."
And then I knew I was still in my uniform.

Well, I've told you now. They tell you now at eighteen.
There's no use telling before.
                Do you understand?
That's why we have the Ritual of the Earth,
The Day of Sorrow, the other ceremonies.
Oh, yes, at first people hated the animals
Because they still bred, but we've gotten over that.
Perhaps they can work it better, when it's their turn,
If it's their turn—I don't know. I don't know at all.
You can call it a virus, of course, if you like the word,
But we haven't been able to find it. Not yet. No.
It isn't as if it had happened all at once.
There were a few children born in the last six months
Before the end of the war, so there's still some hope.
But they're almost grown. That's the trouble. They're almost
    grown.

Well, we had a long run. That's something. At first they thought
There might be a nation somewhere—a savage tribe.
But we were all in it, even the Eskimos,
And we keep the toys in the stores, and the colored books,
And people marry and plan and the rest of it,
But, you see, there aren't any children. They aren't born.

[1938]

The Voice of the Dolphins

The Voice of the Dolphins

O<small>N SEVERAL OCCASIONS</small> between 1960 and 1985, the world narrowly escaped an all-out atomic war. In each case, the escape was due more to fortuitous circumstances than to the wisdom of the policies pursued by statesmen.

That the bomb would pose a novel problem to the world was clear as early as 1946. It was not clearly recognized, however, that the solution of this problem would involve political and technical considerations in an inseparable fashion. In America, few statesmen were aware of the technical considerations, and, prior to Sputnik, only few scientists were aware of the political considerations. After Sputnik, Dr. James R. Killian was appointed by President Eisenhower, on a full-time basis, as chairman of the President's Science Advisory Committee, and, thereafter, a number of distinguished scientists were drawn into the work of the Committee and became aware of all aspects of the problem posed by the bomb.

Why, then, one may ask, did scientists in general, and the President's Science Advisory Committee in particular, fail to advance a solution of this problem during the Eisenhower administration? The slogan that "scientists should be on tap but not on top," which gained currency in Washington, may have had something to do with this failure. Of course, scientists could not possibly be on top in Washington, where policy, if it is made at all, is made by those who operate, rather than by those who are engaged in policy planning. But what those who coined this slogan, and those who parroted it, apparently meant was that scientists must not concern themselves with devising and proposing policies; they ought to limit themselves to answering such technical questions as they may be asked. Thus, it may well be that the scientists gave the wrong answers because they were asked the wrong questions.

In retrospect, it would appear that among the various recommendations made by the President's Science Advisory Committee there was only one which has borne fruit. At some point or other, the Committee had recommended that there be set up, at the opportune time, a major joint Russian-American research project having no relevance to the national defense, or to any politically controversial issues. The setting up in 1963 of the Biological Research Institute in Vienna under a contract between the Russian and American governments was in line with this general recommendation of the Committee.

20

When the Vienna Institute came to be established, both the American and the Russian molecular biologists manifested a curious predilection for it. Because most of those who applied for a staff position were distinguished scientists, even though comparatively young, practically all of those who applied were accepted.

This was generally regarded at that time as a major setback for this young branch of science, in Russia as well as in America, and there were those who accused Sergei Dressler of having played the role of the Pied Piper. There may have been a grain of truth in this accusation, inasmuch as a conference on molecular biology held in Leningrad in 1962 was due to his initiative. Dressler spent a few months in America in 1960 surveying the advances in molecular biology. He was so impressed by what he saw that he decided to do something to stimulate this new branch of science in his native Russia. The Leningrad Conference was attended by many Americans; it was the first time that American and Russian molecular biologists came into contact with each other, and the friendships formed on this occasion were to last a lifetime.

When the first scientific communications came out of the Vienna Institute, it came as a surprise to everyone that they were not in the field of molecular biology, but concerned themselves with the intellectual capacity of the dolphins.

That the organization of the brain of the dolphin has a complexity comparable to that of man had been known for a long time. In 1960, Dr. John C. Lilly reported that the dolphins might have a language of their own, that they were capable of imitating human speech and that the intelligence of the dolphins might be equal to that of humans, or possibly even superior to it. This report made enough of a stir, at that time, to hit the front pages of the newspapers. Subsequent attempts to learn the language of the dolphins, to communicate with them and to teach them, appeared to be discouraging, however, and it was generally assumed that Dr. Lilly had overrated their intelligence.

In contrast to this view, the very first bulletin from the Vienna Institute took the position that previous failures to communicate with the dolphins might not have been due to the dolphins' lack of intellectual capacity but rather to their lack of motivation. In a second communiqué the Vienna Institute disclosed that the dolphins proved to be extraordinarily fond of Sell's liver paste, that they became quickly addicted to it and that the expectation of being rewarded by being fed this particular brand of liver paste could motivate them to perform intellectually strenuous tasks.

A number of subsequent communiqués from the Institute concerned themselves with objectively determining the exact limit of the intellectual capacity of the dolphins. These communiqués gradually revealed that their intelligence far surpassed that of man. However, on account of their submerged mode of life, the dolphins were ignorant of facts, and thus they had not been able to put their intelligence to good use in the past.

Having learned the language of the dolphins and established communication with them, the staff of the Institute began to teach them first mathematics, next chemistry and physics, and subsequently biology. The dolphins acquired knowledge in all of these fields with extraordinary rapidity. Because of their lack of manual dexterity the dolphins were not able to perform experiments. In time, however, they began to suggest to the staff experiments in the biological field, and soon thereafter it became apparent that the staff of the Institute might be relegated to performing experiments thought up by the dolphins.

During the first three years of the operation of the Institute all of its publications related to the intellectual capacity of the dolphins. The communiqués issued in the fourth year, five in number, were, however, all in the field of molecular biology. Each one of these communiqués reported a major advance in this field and was issued not in the name of the staff members who had actually performed the experiment, but in the name of the dolphins who had suggested it. (At the time when they were brought into the Institute the dolphins were each designated by a Greek syllable, and they retained these designations for life.)

Each of the next five Nobel Prizes for physiology and medicine was awarded for one or another of these advances. Since it was legally impossible, however, to award the Nobel Prize to a dolphin, all the awards were made to the Institute as a whole. Still, the credit went, of course, to the dolphins, who derived much prestige from these awards, and their prestige was to increase further in the years to come, until it reached almost fabulous proportions.

In the fifth year of its operation, the Institute isolated a mutant form of a strain of commonly occurring algae, which excreted a broad-spectrum antibiotic and was able to fix nitrogen. Because of these two characteristics, these algae could be grown in the open, in improvised ditches filled with water, and they did not require the addition of any nitrates as fertilizer. The protein extracted from them had excellent nutritive qualities and a very pleasant taste.

The algae, the process of growing them and the process of extracting their protein content, as well as the protein product itself, were patented by the Institute, and when the product was marketed—under the trade name Amruss—the Institute collected royalties.

If taken as a protein substitute in adequate quantities, Amruss markedly depresses the fertility of women, but it has no effect on the fertility of men. Amruss seemed to be the answer to the prayer of countries like India. India had a severe immediate problem of food shortage; and she had an equally severe long-term problem, because her population had been increasing at the rate of five million a year.

Amruss sold at about one tenth of the price of soybean protein, and in the first few years of its production the demand greatly exceeded the supply. It also raised a major problem for the Catholic Church. At first Rome took no official position on the consumption of Amruss by Catholics, but left it to each individual bishop to issue such ruling for his diocese as he deemed advisable. In Puerto Rico the Catholic Church simply chose to close an eye. In a number of South American countries, however, the bishops took the position that partaking of Amruss was a mortal sin, no different from other forms of contraception.

In time, this attitude of the bishops threatened to have serious consequences for the Church, because it tended to undermine the institution of the confession. In countries such as El Salvador, Ecuador, Nicaragua and Peru, women gradually got tired of confessing again and again to having committed a mortal sin, and of being told again and again to do penance; in the end they simply stopped going to confession.

When the decline in the numbers of those who went to confession became conspicuous, it came to the attention of the Pope. As is generally known, in the end the issue was settled by the papal bull "Food Being Essential for Maintaining Life," which stressed that Catholics ought not to be expected to starve when food was available. Thereafter, bishops uniformly took the position that Amruss was primarily a food, rather than a contraceptive.

The income of the Institute, from the royalties collected, rapidly increased from year to year, and within a few years it came to exceed the subsidies from the American and Russian governments. Because the Institute had internationally recognized tax-free status, the royalties were not subject to tax.

The first investment made by the Vienna Institute was the purchase of television stations in a number of cities all over the world. Thereafter, the television programs of these stations carried no advertising. Since they no longer had to aim their programs at the largest possible audience, there was no longer any need for them to cater to the taste of morons. This freedom from the need of maximizing their audience led to a rapid evolution of the art of television, the potential of which had been frequently surmised but never actually realized.

One of the major television programs carried by the Amruss stations was devoted to the discussion of political problems. The function of The Voice of the Dolphins, as this program was called, was to clarify what the real issues were. In taking up an issue, The Voice would discuss what the several possible solutions were and would indicate in each case what the price of that particular solution might be. A booklet circulated by The Voice of the Dolphins explained why the program set itself this particular task, as follows:

Political issues were often complex, but they were rarely anywhere as deep as the scientific problems which had been solved in the first half of the century. These scientific problems had been solved with amazing rapidity because they had been constantly exposed to discussion among scientists, and thus it appeared reasonable to expect that the solution of political problems could be greatly speeded up also if they were subjected to the same kind of discussion. The discussions of political problems by politicians were much less productive, because they differed in one important respect from the discussions of scientific problems by scientists: When a scientist says something, his colleagues must ask themselves only whether it is true. When a politician says something, his colleagues must first of all ask, "Why does he say it?"; later on they may or may not get around to asking whether it happens to be true. A politician is a man who thinks he is in possession of the truth and knows what needs to be done; thus his only problem is to persuade people to do what needs to be done. Scientists rarely think that they are in full possession of the truth, and a scientist's aim in a discussion with his colleagues is not to persuade but to clarify. It was clarification rather than persuasion that was needed in the past to arrive at the solution of the great scientific problems.

Because the task of The Voice was to clarify rather than to persuade, The Voice did not provide political leadership, but by clarifying what the issues were in the field of politics The Voice made it possible for intellectual leadership to arise in this field.

A number of political scientists were invited to join the Institute at the time when The Voice of the Dolphins went into operation, and the first suggestion of the dolphins in the political field was made one year later. At that time, the dolphins proposed that the United Nations set up a commission in every South American capital and that these commissions function along the lines of the U. N. Commission that had been in operation in Bolivia since 1950. That commission was advising the Bolivian government on all matters pertaining to the economic welfare of the nation; in addition, it made available trained personnel on whom the Bolivian government could draw, if it wanted to put into effect any of the commission's recommendations.

This proposal of the dolphins was generally regarded as wholly unrealistic. It was pointed out that the governments of the South American nations did not operate in a vacuum, but were subject to political pressures from private interests. It was freely predicted, therefore, that any attempt on the part of a U.N. commission to influence the action of the government to which it was accredited would be frustrated by the influence of the private interests, no matter how sound the advice might be. But such was the prestige of the dolphins that their proposal, formally submitted to the United Nations by Uruguay, was adopted by a two-thirds majority of the General Assembly, after it had been vetoed in the Security Council.

Still, the skeptics might well have turned out to be right, had it not been for the activities of the "special agencies" which the Vienna Institute established in every one of the South American capitals where a U.N. commission was in operation. Even though these special agencies had no policy of their own other than to support the proposals of the local United Nations commissions, and even though they operated on a rather limited budget—none spent more than $15 million a year—without their activities the U.N. commissions could not have achieved their ambitious goals in South America. The amounts which these "special agencies" spent, small though they were, were effective because they were spent exclusively for the purpose of bribing the members of the government in office to do what was in the public interest, rather than to yield to the pressures of private interests.

Had it not been for the extra income that the Vienna Institute derived from the sale of Amruss, its activities would have come to an end in 1970, at the time of the Communist revolution in Iraq, when all Russian-American contracts were canceled and the Institute lost its government subsidies.

In order to make the subsequent events fully understandable to the reader it is necessary to make him aware of the change that the character of the so-called atomic stalemate underwent between 1960 and 1970.

Between 1962 and 1965 the world passed through an agonizing transitional phase in the atomic stalemate. At the beginning of this period America had still to rely mostly on

27

bombers, based on airfields located in the proximity of Russia. Because of the possibility of a surprise attack which could have knocked out America's ability to strike a counterblow, the United States felt impelled to keep one third of her bombers in the air on an around-the-clock basis in times of crisis. Russia, on the other hand, had no foreign bases, nor was she in need of any, since she possessed an adequate stockpile of long-range rockets which could be launched from bases inside Russia and were capable of carrying hydrogen bombs large enough to demolish a city. By 1965 America had an adequate stockpile of such long-range rockets also, and thereafter she was no longer in need of foreign bases, either.

By 1965 America and Russia were capable of destroying each other to any desired degree. They both had long-range rockets mounted on trucks or railroad cars that were kept constantly on the move, and it would have been impossible for either country to destroy, by one single sudden blow, the power of the other to strike a devastating counterblow. With the fear of a surprise attack thus eliminated, the atomic stalemate began to gain a stability which it did not formerly possess.

At a time when America and Russia could have destroyed each other to any desired degree, the threat of massive retaliation would have been tantamount to a threat of murder and suicide. Such a threat might be believable if it were made by a nation in a conflict in which its very existence was at stake, but it would not be believable if it were made by America in a conflict in which American interests were at stake, but not America's existence as a nation. In these circumstances America ceased to rely on long-range rockets and the large bomb for the defense of her national interests in case of an armed conflict. Instead, America planned to send troops to the area involved and to resist by using small atomic bombs against troops in combat, within the contested area.

28

In time, people in America came to understand well enough that the "real aim" of such a limited war could not be victory, which clearly would not be obtainable in every case, but, rather, the exacting of a price from the enemy. It was thought that if America were able to exact a price higher than the price which the enemy would be prepared to pay, then America's ability to fight a limited atomic war anywhere on the globe would effectively deter the enemy from attempting to change the map by force. It was recognized, of course, that America might have to be prepared to pay a price as high as she proposed to exact, not only in money but perhaps also in lives—the lives of the young men who would die in the fighting.

It was generally taken for granted that the large bombs and the long-range rockets would play no role in any of the foreseeable conflicts. They were kept as an insurance for the sole purpose of retaliating if Russia were to attack America with such bombs.

No one had any doubt that the revolution in Iraq, which caught America by surprise in 1970, was in fact Communist-inspired, and America responded promptly by landing troops in Lebanon and Jordan. This time America was determined to settle the issue of control of the Middle East and thus to end, once and for all, the threat that Western Europe might be cut off from its Middle East oil supply. Egypt and Syria declared that they would regard an invasion of Iraq by American troops as an attack against themselves. Turkish troops were poised to move into Syria, and Russia was concentrating troops on the Turkish border, for the purpose of restraining Turkey.

At this point America proclaimed that she was prepared to send troops into Turkey, to use small atomic bombs in combat against Russian troops on Turkish soil and, perhaps,

THE VOICE OF THE DOLPHINS

also in hot pursuit beyond the prewar Turkish-Russian boundary.

It appeared that Russia strongly disliked the prospect of fighting an atomic war on her southern border. There was little assurance that such a war would not spread and finally end up in an all-out war, and rather than to take this risk Russia decided to adopt a strategy of another kind. In a note, which was kept very short, she proclaimed that she would not resist by force of arms in the Middle East an American invasion of that area, but would, rather, seek to "deter" America by setting a high price for such an invasion. The price would be set, however, not in terms of human life but solely in terms of property.

The Russian note listed twelve American cities by name. Russia stated that if American troops crossed over into Iraq she would single out one of these twelve cities, give that city four weeks of warning to permit its orderly evacuation, as well as to allow time to make arrangements for the feeding and housing of refugees, and thereafter the city would be demolished with one single long-range rocket.

America replied in a note which was even shorter and intimated that for each city that Russia demolished in America, America would demolish two cities in Russia.

To this Russia replied in a second note—a note of unprecedented length—that if America were to demolish two cities in Russia for each city that Russia might have demolished in America, and if Russia were to demolish two cities in America for each city that America might have demolished in Russia, then the destruction of even one city would trigger a chain of events which would, step by step, lead to the destruction of all American as well as all Russian cities. Since clearly America could not possibly want this result, she should not make such a threat of "two for one" and expect it to be believed. Russia, on her part, would tolerate America's

30

protest against Russia's supplying oil at cut-rate prices to Western Europe, thus demonstrating once more that the capitalist nations have no monopoly in feuding with each other.

Russia did derive great economic benefits from her decision to forgo war. In short order, she abolished her Air Force and her entire Navy, including her fleet of submarines; she also reduced her Army and retained only a comparatively small number of highly mobile units equipped with machine guns and light tanks. Russia continued to maintain, of course, a large number of long-range rockets mounted on trucks or on railroad cars, which were constantly moved around along her highways and railroad tracks.

As the result of the economies thus achieved, Russia was able to invest 25 per cent of her national income in capital goods serving her consumer-goods industry, and her standard of living was increasing at the rate of 8 per cent per annum. Her per capita consumption of meats and fats rapidly approached that of America; as a result, deaths from coronary attacks rose very markedly and were approaching the American figures.

Propagandawise the Russians stressed the moral issue involved and made the most of it. All over the world Communists and Russian sympathizers proclaimed that wars, which initially merely meant the killing of soldiers, but in the end came to mean the wholesale killing of civilians—men, women and children—as well as soldiers, were now a thing of the past, thanks to Russia's decision to forgo, abrogate and abolish war. They said, over and over again, that Russia was the only truly Christian nation, since she alone, among the Great Powers, was upholding the Fifth Commandment.*

---

* The possibility that it might be to Russia's advantage to adopt this type of strategy was discussed by Szilard in an extensive article which appeared in the February issue of the Bulletin of the

demolishing one Russian city, in return for Russia's having demolished one American city. But for each additional city that America might demolish, Russia would demolish one and just one additional city in America.

The note made it clear that even though Russia would abide by such a principle of "one for one," this did not mean that America would be free to demolish a large city in Russia in return for a small city demolished in America. What would count in this respect, the note stated, would be the size of the city, as expressed by the number of inhabitants rather than by the number of square miles covered by the city.

Twenty-four hours after this Russian note was received in Washington, the Division of Vital Statistics of the Vienna Institute issued a document which listed the number of inhabitants of all American and all Russian cities. In their preface the dolphins stated that if American troops were to invade Iraq, and Russia were to demolish one of the twelve cities she had listed, an undesirable controversy might arise on the issue of which American city was equal to which Russian city, unless an authentic list of the number of inhabitants was readily available.

This document was issued so promptly that it aroused Russian suspicion. The Russians thought that somehow the Vienna Institute might have had inside information about Russian intentions and thus been able to prepare in advance this list of cities. American and British statesmen had so often said that the Russians were unpredictable that finally the Russians themselves came to believe it. There is no reason, however, to think that the Vienna Institute had any advance information. Rather, it seems that the dolphins, being not inferior in intelligence to the men in Moscow who devised Russia's policies, were frequently able to predict the moves that Russia would make. This view is borne out by the few records of the Vienna Institute which survived the fire that destroyed the Institute in 1990.

The second Russian note caused a turmoil in Washington. Various groups urged that the Government adopt a rigid policy of demolishing two Russian cities for each city demolished in America, or that it accept the principle of "one for one," or that it do neither, but just keep the Russians guessing.

At a meeting of the National Security Council several public-relations experts expressed the view that were Russia actually to demolish one of the twelve cities she had listed, the public would demand that America retaliate by demolishing a number of Russian cities. They said that the President would thus not be able to abide by the principle of "one for one," even if he desired to do so, without seriously risking the defeat of his party at the next elections.

The Government thereupon asked Gallup to conduct a poll on an emergency basis. Residents of the thirty largest cities were asked whether if Rochester, New York, one of the twelve cities named, were demolished, America ought to retaliate by demolishing just one Russian city, or whether she ought to retaliate by demolishing a number of Russian cities. To the surprise of the Government, 85 per cent of those who had an opinion favored the demolishing of just one Russian city. In retrospect, this response does not appear to be so very surprising; the people polled knew very well that if America were to demolish two Russian cities in retaliation for Rochester, Russia would demolish one additional American city—and this additional city might be their own.

Some of the members of the National Security Council declined to take this poll at its face value and said that the people would react differently if Rochester were actually demolished. The rather involved psychological argument they

cited in support of their view was never put to a test, however, for America did not intervene in Iraq.

Within a few days after the receipt of the first Russian note which listed the twelve cities, people began to register in Washington as lobbyists for one or another of the twelve cities, and ten days later there was not a hotel room to be had in the whole city. It was the most powerful lobby that ever hit Washington. After an initial period of uncertainty, this lobby succeeded, with steadily increasing editorial support across the nation, in forcing a re-examination of the whole Middle Eastern issue. Doubts were raised as to whether Western Europe was really in danger of losing its supply of Middle Eastern oil, since there was no other market for it. It was said that while the price of oil from the Middle East could be raised, it could not be raised very much, since it could be replaced by oil from the Sahara. As the result of a re-examination of the whole issue, America decided to withdraw her troops from Lebanon and Jordan.

This decision was reached in the face of strenuous opposition on the part of a small, but vocal and influential, group of opinion makers. There were prophets of doom who declared that if America yielded to Russia's threat on this occasion, then from here on Russia would be in a position to get her way on any issue; she would be in a position to change the map at will, simply by threatening to demolish a limited number of American cities, in case America should try to resist locally, by force of arms.

Fortunately these prophecies proved to be incorrect. For the time being, at least, Russia appeared to be quite satisfied with the map as it stood. True enough, a number of nations in Southeast Asia went Communist, and so did several nations in Africa. On the other hand, the Communist government of Iraq broke diplomatic relations with Russia, in

Following the Iraq crisis there were two rival schools of thought in America.

One of these held that America ought to follow Russia's example: cut down on her arms expenditure by reducing the Army, the Navy and the Air Force and adopt the Russian strategy of relying on long-range rockets.

The other school argued that operating with the threat of demolishing cities would favor Russia rather than America, because the American government was more responsible to the will of the people and the people did not like to see their cities demolished. They urged, therefore, that an all-out effort be made to develop an antimissile missile, capable of destroying incoming Russian rockets in flight, and stressed that a defense system based on such missiles would nullify the Russian strategy of demolishing cities.

The President's Science Advisory Committee took a dim view of the feasibility of an effective antimissile defense system, but in the end the views of the Department of De-

---

Atomic Scientists in 1960. It is not known whether Szilard's article elicited any response other than a notice in Newsweek, in America, and in Krokodil, in Russia. Newsweek condensed this article beyond recognition and managed to convey the impression that Szilard proposed that Russia and America ought to demolish each other's cities in exchange—to no sensible purpose. Taking its information from Newsweek, Krokodil suggested in its issue of April 20, 1960, that Newsweek carry an ad for Szilard offering to exchange his Room 812 in the Medical Division of Memorial Hospital in New York for a bed in Ward 6 in the Psychiatric Division of the same hospital. Some of his American colleagues do remember that Szilard made a prediction concerning the strategy which the Russians would adopt if there were no general disarmament, but they remember only that he predicted something rather crazy, without recalling what it was that he predicted. After his death, Szilard appears to have received some recognition, however, from his Russian colleagues, who named a small crater after him—on the back side of the moon.

fense prevailed; thus, an appropriation of $20 billion per year for the development of such a defense system was included in the budget and unanimously passed by Congress.

Most of those who urged the development of the anti-missile missile also urged that America cease to rely on atomic bombs used against troops in combat and be fully prepared to fight limited wars with conventional weapons. They argued, convincingly, that a war in which atomic weapons were used against troops in combat would not be likely to remain limited and might end up in all-out atomic destruction. Since the enemy must know this also—so they further argued—it would not resort to the use of atomic bombs against troops in combat as long as America limited herself to fighting with conventional weapons.

Taking its cues from this school of thought, the American government adopted the position that it would be immoral to use atomic energy for purposes of destruction and urged that all use of atomic bombs in warfare be outlawed. The government proposed that, until such time as atomic bombs can be eliminated from the armaments of the nations under satisfactory safeguards, each nation pledge unilaterally not to use atomic bombs either against troops in combat or for the purposes of destruction. If such pledges were given, then America would use only in retaliation the atomic bombs it retained, and only if America or one of her allies were attacked with atomic bombs.

The position of the American government was generally supported by the press. Noted columnists pointed out that even though outlawing the atomic bomb would not necessarily prevent the use of such bombs in time of war, it would preclude nations from resorting to the threat of using atomic bombs in order to attain their objectives.

The American proposal that the use of atomic bombs be

36

outlawed represented the main theme of most of the programs of *The Voice of America*, which received an appropriation of $1 billion a year, and the American proposal for out-
lawing the bomb received world-wide support. But even
though during the postwar period the outlawing of the bomb
had been persistently urged by Russia, the Russians showed
no interest in this approach. They stood fast in the face of
adverse world public opinion, and no indication was forth-
coming that Russia would go along with outlawing the use of
atomic energy for purposes of destruction.

Pending the completion of the development of the antimissile missile, America followed a triple policy of maintaining long-range rockets to be used in retaliation in case America were attacked by means of such rockets, a small but
mobile military force equipped to use small atomic bombs
against troops in combat, and also a large combat-ready military force capable of fighting local wars by means of conventional weapons. Since maintaining such a triple system
was costly, America had an arms budget of around $70 bil-
lion. This cut down the amount invested in capital goods
serving the consumer goods industry to about 3 per cent of
the national income, and it slowed the rise in the standard of
living to about one per cent per annum. Such a stagnation in
the standard of living was not a very serious detriment, however, since the standard of living was high enough as it stood;
moreover, a high defense expenditure was regarded as an
insurance against the possibility of a recession.

The depression which hit America in 1974 began with
unemployment in the construction industry, which subsequently spread to other industries. In the hope of inducing
the Federal government to finance large-scale construction,
the construction industry established a lobby in Washington
in the second year of the depression. But, in spite of large-

scale Federal construction, there was no marked economic improvement by 1977, at the time when America was confronted with upheavals in Iran.

The Government responded to these upheavals by promptly proclaiming that if Russia should send troops into Iran, America would not fight her in Iran, but, instead, two Russian cities of about one million each would be demolished, after being given four weeks of warning. People knew, of course, that should Russia actually invade Iran, not only Russia but also America would lose two cities, but it was generally felt that, because of the large-scale unemployment prevailing in the construction industry, America would be in a position to rebuild, in short order, the cities which she might lose.

In these circumstances, the government's proclamation had strong support in Congress, and it would be uncalled for to attribute this solely to the influence of the lobby of the construction industry. Congressmen might very well have realized that, with the development of the antimissile missile still lagging, the government had no other recourse but to adopt the so-called "Russian strategy."

Russia did not send troops into Iran. Whether she refrained from doing so because she would have lost two of her cities or whether she never had any serious intention of becoming involved in the mess in Iran may be regarded today as debatable. At that time, however, the press in America stressed that the Russians had an emotional attitude toward property and abhorred the destruction of property, particularly public property. They also stressed that the loss of a city would mean more to Russia than just the loss of property, that it would disrupt the social fabric and cause dislocations which the precariously balanced Russian social system could not easily stand.

The Iranian incident was followed by a period of quiet, and many people began to believe that the strategic stalemate had reached a stage where it was virtually stable. The map appeared to be frozen, at least in the sense that such changes as came about came about through genuine internal revolutions and no nation sent its troops across the frontier of another nation in an attempt to increase the territory under its control.

Around 1980, however, there appeared a new kind of instability, which developed into a serious threat to the world by 1985. In order to understand the problems that confronted the world in that critical year, it is necessary to consider how the world situation had changed in the interval from 1960 to 1985.

THE AMERICAN RESEARCH FOUNDATION

The years that followed the Second World War brought unprecedented changes in the Far East. What was really novel and unique about China was not so much that China had a Communist government, but that for the first time since the days of the emperors China had a government. By 1960, it was clear that the Chinese would be able to raise production greatly, but it was not as yet clear whether at the time when this would become necessary they would be able to slow the rate of their population increase. Had they failed in this, no amount of economic progress, within the limits of the obtainable, could have appreciably raised their standard of living. It is anyone's guess whether China would have succeeded in solving her population problem had it not been for the replacement of much of her rice diet by a diet of Amruss.

It seems that by 1960 most Americans realized the foolishness of opposing the seating of China in the UN and of pursuing a policy of "No Speak" toward China. Szilard's diary, recently reprinted by Simon and Schuster, contains an entry made in 1960 to the effect that he did not know personally anyone who still thought that America ought to persist in opposing the seating of China in the United Nations. In flagrant contrast to this, virtually all of those who ran for elective office in that year went on record against the seating of China.

This is not so surprising as it might seem, if one recalls to what extent the American two-party system favors minority rule. A few per cent of the voters who feel strongly enough on an issue to be willing to throw their vote, on that single issue, from the Democratic to the Republican candidate or vice versa, may well be in a position to determine which of the two candidates shall win. This explains why, under the American political system, a minority may force its will on the nation as a whole. Thus America's long-sustained opposition to the seating of China in the UN was forced upon her by an emotional minority of the voters, representing less than 5 per cent of the votes.

America never actually changed her vote on the issue of the seating of China in the United Nations, but she was outvoted by a two-thirds majority in the General Assembly. She refused to recognize China until 1966. That the dolphins had anything to do with America's recognition of China in 1966 was not known at the time, for people did not realize that the dolphins exerted a decisive influence on this issue through the American Research Foundation.

This foundation derived its income from the Vienna Institute, and its income exceeded that of the Ford Foundation twentyfold. The trustees of the foundation, apparently handpicked by the dolphins, served on a part-time basis, without salary. Membership on the Advisory Board of the foundation was, however, a full-time job carrying a salary of $200,000 a year for life. When, in the course of the years, the Advisory Board was built up to full strength its membership consisted of twenty distinguished politicians, Democrats and Republicans in about equal numbers.

The first politician to join the advisory board was Peter Douglas, who became Secretary of State when the new Administration took office following the 1964 elections. Douglas, who was irrevocably opposed to the recognition of China, resigned his position as Secretary of State in June 1965 to accept a life membership on the advisory board. His successor in office was Roger Knowland,* a Californian, who was also strongly opposed to the recognizing of China. He, in turn, resigned his office in February 1966 to join the Advisory Board. His successor as Secretary of State, Milton Land, former Senator from Massachusetts, did not share the views of his predecessors, and the U. S. finally recognized China.

According to the charter of the American Research Foundation, the Advisory Board wielded great power, for its recommendations were supposed to be binding on the board of trustees. However, the charter also specified that these recommendations must be passed by a unanimous vote, and it seems that no resolution ever passed the Advisory Board by unanimous vote. While this must have been rather frustrating to its members, there is no record of anyone's ever having resigned from the general advisory board.

It is quite evident—in retrospect—that membership on the Advisory Board had never been offered by the foundation to any Cabinet officer or any member of the Senate who pursued, or supported, a constructive foreign policy. It should be borne in mind, however, that only in the light of subse-

---

* No relation of the late Senator William Knowland.

quent events could it become evident whether a foreign policy was constructive or not.

In the circumstances, the world might well have remained unaware of the role which the dolphins played in American politics, except for the revelations contained in Alex Gamov's *Conversations with Pi Omega Ro*, (10th edition, New York, Harper and Brothers, 1998), which covers the two years immediately preceding the establishment of the foundation.

There was a time when people thought that the discussions reported in the *Conversations* were transcripts of the conversations which staff members of the Vienna Institute had with Pi Omega Ro. In view of the inconsistencies discovered, this view is probably no longer tenable, and today it is regarded as more likely that Gamov reconstructed these conversations imperfectly from memory.

As the reader may recall, Gamov, a member of the staff of the Vienna Institute, had married the sister of one of his American colleagues and did not return in 1990 to Russia, but joined the Salk Institute in La Jolla, California. Upon his retirement ten years later, he began to write the *Conversations*.

In his book he relates that the dolphins, who grasped mathematics, chemistry, physics and biology with ease, found it difficult to comprehend America's social and political system. The American staff members whose task it was to explain America to Pi Omega Ro were at times so exasperated by the questions asked by this dolphin that they asked Gamov, who spoke flawless English, to come to their rescue.

Thus, on one occasion, Pi Omega Ro asked whether it would be correct to assume that Americans were free to say what they think, because they did not think what they were not free to say. On another occasion, he asked whether it would be correct to say that in America honest politicians

42

were men who were unable to fool others without first fooling themselves.

When Pi Omega Ro became interested in foundations he wanted to know everything about them, including the legal technicalities of their tax exemption. Upon being informed that a tax-exempt foundation may not spend its funds to influence legislation but may spend them on education, he asked whether this implied that in America education did not influence legislation.

Pi Omega Ro was puzzled why money which would otherwise be taxed away and go to the Treasury should be permitted to go to foundations when obviously foundations never did anything worth while except what the Government was doing anyway and, in many cases, was doing better. He regarded the bylaws of the foundations, which provided that grants for research projects be allocated by a simple majority vote of the trustees, as an ingeniously contrived device to make certain that no imaginative project was ever approved. "Let us assume, for the sake of argument," he argued, "that one third of the trustees are men endowed with imagination and two thirds of them are not so endowed. Does not the majority vote then automatically bar any imaginative project? And even if we accept, as the basic tenet of true democracy, that one moron is as good as one genius, is it necessary to go one step farther and hold that two morons are better than one genius?"

These conversations must be regarded as authentic, in spite of the doubts which were raised by some of Gamov's colleagues who knew him at La Jolla. Their observation that Pi Omega Ro's sense of humor showed a remarkable resemblance to Gamov's own sense of humor is of no relevance, since his long association with Pi Omega Ro may well have colored Gamov's own sense of humor. The *Conversations*

43

is the only authentic document that reveals that from its inception the foundation meant to influence the course of political events in America and that the dolphins knew that no politician would be able to resist the offer of a membership on the Advisory Board.)

THE FAR EAST AND EUROPE, 1960 TO 1985

The American attitude toward China started to change even before the U. S. recognized China.

As the world moved closer and closer to the long-range-rocket stage of the stalemate, nations like France, Italy, Western Germany and Japan realized more and more clearly that they could not count on American protection if they got involved in a war with Russia, because America could hardly be expected to risk the loss of her own cities for the sake of protecting theirs. This consideration led to an increasingly strong demand on the part of these nations to have hydrogen bombs under their own control. America might have resisted these demands had it not been for the fact that by then America had begun to look upon her allies more and more as potential liabilities rather than potential assets. Therefore, in order to free herself from any moral commitment to defend her allies, America felt inclined to provide them with bombs which they could use in their own defense.

Shortly after America undertook to provide France, Germany, Italy and Japan with their own bombs, Russia decided to provide China with the bombs that China felt she needed for her security. The Central African Federation, which was initially formed to constitute a non-nuclear block, was not provided with bombs and rockets until about ten years later.

Soon after China became an atomic power, there was a

44

marked change in the American attitude on the issue of the islands of Quemoy and Matsu. Up to that time, for reasons of expediency, the American press had egged on the Chinese Nationalists to hold on to these islands. Thereafter, however, it was said with increasing frequency that it would be morally wrong for America to encourage the Nationalists to persist in the occupation of these offshore islands.

But just about the time when American policy toward China became more conciliatory, the Chinese attitude began to harden. When the Chinese population ceased to increase rapidly, the standard of living began to rise in China, and, with increasing prosperity, there was an increase in China's expansionist tendencies. This is quite understandable, even though it is the exact opposite of what people had generally predicted. Invariably people who believe that they are in possession of the truth wish to spread the gospel, and for a while the Chinese believed that they were in possession of the truth.

But, just as the zest of British imperialism persisted only as long as the English thought that by extending their system to other nations they could bring them the blessings of "civilization," thus also the expansionist tendencies of China persisted only until the Chinese found that they were unable to bring about a betterment of the lot of the Indians by imposing on India the blessings of the Communist system.

It is curious that India, of all nations, should play this role of bringing disenchantment to imperialism. It is even more curious that she should play this role twice within the century and under such very different circumstances. No one has done more to disenchant British imperialism than did Gandhi, and he did it because he was the incarnation of the highest virtues of the Indians. However, the disenchantment that India brought to China was not due to any virtues, but, rather, to the absence of virtues.

45

When India became Communist, China went all out to make Communism in India a success, but after ten years of Communist rule in India it began to dawn on the Chinese that the success of their own regime in China may have been to a large extent due to the civic virtues of the Chinese, which the Indians were totally lacking. The recognition of this greatly increased China's national pride, but at the same time it decreased her zeal to extend her political system to other nations.

After Chiang Kai-shek's untimely death, the "Formosa for Formosans" movement began to gather strength rather rapidly. Formosa had been separated from China for two generations, and Formosans liked neither the Chinese on the mainland nor those who had come to Formosa from the mainland. There were rumors that the American government secretly encouraged the "Formosa for Formosans" movement. There is no evidence, however, that any government funds were in fact involved, even though funds for cultural activities may have come from private sources in the United States, such as the Rockefeller Cousins' Fund.

After a while the situation became rather uncomfortable for the remnants of the Chinese Nationalists on Formosa, and most of them wanted to leave that island. China had a severe shortage of clerical workers and offered asylum to all those born on the mainland; a law enacted by the United States Congress made it possible for those of them who wanted to come to America to do so, provided they did not intend to take up residence in California.

Most people expected that China would thereafter occupy Formosa, but China appeared to have somehow lost interest in Formosa. The Americans, the English, the Germans and the Russians have always been regarded as barbarians by the Chinese, and the Japanese have been looked upon as semi-civilized. Formosa had been under Japanese rule for two generations, and apparently the Chinese came to regard the native Formosans as no more civilized than the Japanese.

When it became manifest that China was not interested in Formosa any longer, the stage was set for a political settlement in the Far East and the freezing of the map of Southeast Asia.

At the same time, however, a political settlement in Europe appeared to be as far off as ever. In Germany, united since 1980, the Social Democrats, being the largest party in the parliament, were in office. But there were four parties holding seats in the German parliament, and the position of the Government was precarious. All Germans were united in their determination to recover from Poland the territories which Germany had lost to her at the end of the Second World War, but there was violent disagreement among the political parties as to the method of accomplishing this. The Social Democrats and the Christian Democrats wanted to force Poland to return these territories to Germany through negotiations conducted under such economic pressure as Germany was now capable of exerting. The People's Party, however (which had been rapidly increasing in strength and had come to control 45 per cent of the votes in the parliament), advocated the use of force if necessary.

Poland had made it abundantly clear that she would in no circumstances attempt to fight a war on the Polish-German border, and that if German troops were to invade her territory she would exact a high price from Germany by demolishing two German cities, of an unspecified size, for every ten miles' depth of penetration of Polish territory by German troops. Following Russia's classic example, she proclaimed that she would not retaliate if Germany demolished no more than one Polish city of equal size for every city demolished by Poland.

47

The People's Party advocated that Germany should resort to force and should be willing to pay whatever price might be set by the Poles. They argued that Germans, being industrious, as well as prosperous, would be in a better position to rebuild their cities than would the Poles. They contended that the return of the former German territories was not a matter which could be discussed in terms of loss or acquisition of property, because the return of these territories was essential to the spiritual integrity of the German nation.

THE ATOMIC STALEMATE THREATENS
TO BLOW ITSELF UP, 1980 TO 1985

This rather ominous political development in Europe was paralleled by an equally ominous military development the world over. As the Russian rockets increased in numbers and became capable of carrying larger bombs, the situation of the United Kingdom, France, Germany, Italy and Japan became precarious. Up to 1980, these nations had based their security on rockets which were constantly moved around within their territory. However, rockets are guided by delicate instruments, which are ruined if the rockets get badly shaken up. All these countries were small, and had Russia exploded about one fourth of her rockets in a sudden attack, say, over France and Germany, the French and German rockets would have been so badly shaken up that neither of these two countries would have been capable of striking a counterblow. In these circumstances, all the atomic nations, with the exception of America, Russia and China, felt compelled to shift their defense from land-based rockets to rockets based on submarines.

This solved the problem of surprise attack with which these nations were faced, but it created a new problem for the world. If a city were destroyed by a rocket launched from a submarine, it might be possible to trace the orbit of the rocket back to the point at sea from which the rocket had been launched; but with the submarine submerged, it would not be possible to identify the nation responsible for the attack. The possibility of such an anonymous attack was particularly serious in view of the political frustration not only of Germany but also of Japan.

As a result of the high tariffs which America had promulgated to balance her military budget, Japan found herself in economic difficulties, which brought the Japanese militarists into office. The power of China blocked the possibility of a Japanese adventure in Southeast Asia, but Japan, having built a powerful navy, could have moved into the Philippines if America had lost her ability to protect those islands. Thus Japan, though bottled up for the time being, was potentially expansive.

Fears were growing, both in America and in Russia, that one day a bomb might be launched from a German or a Japanese submarine and destroy, say, an American city. Since the identity of the attacker would remain concealed, America might counterattack Russia, with the result that Russia would counterattack America. To what extent such fears were justified it is difficult to say, but it is certain that if Russia and America had mutually destroyed each other this would have left both Germany and Japan in a much better position to pursue their aspirations.*

---

* The reader may recall that, during the Second World War, a few days after Germany went to war against Russia there was an attack from the air against the Hungarian city of Kassa. The Hungarians examined the bomb fragments and found that the bombs were of Russian manufacture. We know today that the bombs were dropped by the German Air Force to create the impression that Russia was the attacker and to induce Hungary to declare war on Russia. This ruse was in fact successful.

49

Apprehensions reached such a level that wealthy Americans went to live in Arizona and New Mexico, where they built luxurious homes equipped with air-conditioned shelters capable of storing a year's food supply, and with attics complete with machine guns mounted in the windows. Many Americans transferred funds to Switzerland, and this movement of funds reached such proportions that Swiss banks ceased to pay interest on deposits and levied a 2 per cent annual "carrying charge."

This flight of capital forced America to raise the price of gold. Ostensibly America did this in order to render economic help to South Africa, where, as the result of a revolution, an all-black government took over, which America was quick to recognize. In fact, however, the chief beneficiary of the rise in the gold price was Russia. Up to then Russia had refrained from exporting gold at the prevailing low prices, and she had begun of late to line the walls of her public toilets with sheets of gold, in token fulfillment of a prophecy once made by Lenin.

In the 1984 elections, civilian defense was a major political issue. The voters were split between those who favored a $10-billion-a-year program of building bomb shelters and those who opposed this but advocated a Federal law that would make it compulsory for all cities above 100,000 population to hold evacuation drills once a year. Once a year, on the appointed day, all the people of such cities would leave the city for a week to be sheltered and fed during that period in the surrounding countryside, at a distance of at least twenty miles from the center of the city. The new Democratic Administration which took office on January 20, 1985, was split on this issue, and so was Congress, with a minority of the Democrats and most of the Republicans opposed to compulsory evacuation drills. But after two Cabinet members, two Senators and one Congressman, who were most effectively opposing the institution of such evacuation drills, resigned their offices in order to become members of the Advisory Board of the American Research Foundation, Congress passed a law providing for once-a-year evacuation drills, which became the law of the land.

The evacuation drill for New York City was set for December 12, 1985, and it caused considerable resentment against the Democratic Administration in Washington because of the heavy losses in Christmas shopping suffered by the retail trade. The evacuation date was set by the mayor of the city, who was a Republican and who was not slated for re-election. It so happened that this was an exceptionally cold December, and among the eight million evacuees there were over 100,000 suffering from frostbite who required treatment upon their return to the city. Most of the other major cities set the date for their evacuation drills for the spring and early summer, but, even so, the evacuation of these cities was regarded by the inhabitants as a major nuisance.

THE DISARMAMENT AGREEMENT
OF 1988

By the fall of 1986 there was strong sentiment in America for general and total disarmament, and in 1987 the dolphins convened at an informal conference at the Vienna Institute to discuss the possibility of such disarmament.

In order to be able to appraise the contribution made by this conference to the achievement of disarmament, it is necessary to recall the political thinking that prevailed on the subject at that time. This thinking is reflected in articles which appeared over a period of years in the *Bulletin of the*

Atomic Scientists, by American, Russian and Chinese authors.

Most of the American authors favored general and total disarmament. They took it more or less for granted that a world disarmed down to machine guns would be a world at peace, but they were less certain about the feasibility of such disarmament. Some Americans held the view that there would be almost no way to make reasonably certain that bombs and rockets which Russia might want to hide could be detected.

Most of the Russian authors, while favoring, in principle, general and complete disarmament, took the position that such disarmament must follow rather than precede the establishment of an international armed force capable of protecting the smaller nations. The Russians pointed out that an improvised army equipped with machine guns could spring up, so to speak, overnight. If a small nation were invaded by such an improvised army of its neighbor, Russia, having given up her bombs and rockets, would be unable to protect that nation.

American authors did not favor the establishment of an international armed force, presumably because they assumed that such an armed force would be set up under the United Nations, where America might be outvoted.

More and more often America was forced to use her veto in the Security Council. The Russians frequently accused America of misusing the veto, but no Russian has ever been able to define the difference between the use of the veto and the misuse of it. Also, Russia succeeded with increasing frequency in depriving America of her right to the veto, by managing to shift the controversy—through the "Uniting for Peace" resolution—to the General Assembly, where she was sometimes able to muster a two-thirds majority.

Some American authors suggested that, in place of setting up an international armed force, the nations of the world should enter into a covenant and pledge themselves to apply stringent economic sanctions against an "aggressor." The Russians doubted, however, that nations who entered into such a covenant would live up to their commitments if this entailed paying a high price in terms of their own economic welfare. The Russians reminded the Americans that when Italy attacked Abyssinia it proved to be impossible to embargo the supply of oil to Italy, because American oil interests were opposed to America's participation in such an embargo, and, further, that when Japan attacked China the United States continued to supply oil and scrap iron to Japan until she herself was ready to enter the Second World War.

Concerned with Europe more than with any other continent, the Russians stressed that while Germany was economically integrated with Western Europe, politically she was not; they stressed that Western Europe was incapable of politically restraining Germany from taking armed action against Poland and was not in a position to apply economic sanctions against Germany without suffering staggering economic losses.

The special disarmament number of the *Bulletin of the Atomic Scientists* of May 1986 contained a number of remarkably lucid articles by American, Chinese and Russian authors. No one who reads these articles can doubt that the Americans were willing to go much further toward total disarmament than were the Russians.

The Russians were willing to consider controlled arms limitations, the idea being that, in return for total elimination of all submarines capable of launching rockets, America, Russia and China would cut down the number of their long-range rockets and bombs below the shake-up level* of the

---

* If a sufficiently large number of sufficiently large bombs were detonated at a suitable height above countries like France, Italy

small atomic countries. Apparently this was as far as they were willing to go in the absence of a reliable UN military force.

The Americans wanted to go much further. They stressed that the problem that the bomb posed to the world could be solved only by eliminating the possibility of war between the Great Powers, and that the kind of controlled-arms limitations which the Russians favored would not accomplish this. They drew a sharp distinction between controlled-arms limitations of the kind which the Russians had in mind and virtually total disarmament which would eliminate the possibility of war between the Great Powers.*

This special number of the *Bulletin* reflected the political ideas prevailing on the subject of disarmament in 1987 when the dolphins convened their informal conference at the Vienna Institute. The steering committee of the conference was composed exclusively of staff members of the Institute, and this caused some resentment even though the Institute was careful to explain the reason for being so exclusive. A

---

or Germany, the explosions would shake up the rockets on the ground to the point where their guidance system would be affected and the rockets would become unusable.

* The first disarmament conference of the League of Nations convened in 1926. It happened that Albert Einstein passed through Geneva during this conference, and when the reporters discovered his presence they asked him how he was impressed by the progress the conference was making. "What would you think," Einstein asked, "about a meeting of a town council which is convened because an increasing number of people are knifed to death each night in drunken brawls, and which proceeds to discuss just how long and how sharp shall be the knife that the inhabitants of the city may be permitted to carry?" After a somewhat shocked silence, one of the reporters asked Einstein, "Do you mean to convey that the disarmament conference is bound to fail?" And Einstein said, "Yes, I do."

letter circulated by the Vienna Institute pointed out that because of the time-consuming process of coding and decoding the speech of the dolphins, the dolphins were in no position to participate in the discussions of the conference directly, and that the staff members of the Vienna Institute were the only people who were able to communicate with the dolphins. They would keep the dolphins currently informed of the progress of the discussions, and it was contemplated to adjourn the conference from time to time so as to permit the steering committee to hold extensive consultations with the dolphins.

At the suggestion of Pi Omega Ro, Ro Epsilon Delta and some of the other leading dolphins, the Institute invited to this conference a number of Russian, American and Chinese scientists who advised their governments on policy planning, but no one was invited whose responsibility was to make policy decisions. Because of the political tension in Europe, the conference was generally regarded as badly timed in Russia, and up to the very last minute it was uncertain whether any Russians would turn up. However, the Russians did come, and they came in time to permit the conference to start on schedule.

The keynote of the conference was set by an introductory document prepared by the steering committee. This Introduction took the position that in previous negotiations concerned with the problem of disarmament major difficulties had been encountered because the nations were apprehensive of secret violations of the agreement. These difficulties had appeared almost insurmountable at the time of the ill-fated Geneva negotiations of 1960 because people were thinking in terms of an agreement to which Russia, America and the other Great Powers would be irrevocably committed. If this were the case, then the agreement would have to spell out

55

in detail the methods of inspection, to which all nations must submit. Possible secret evasions are innumerable, however, and as time went on there would arise new forms of evasion which were not previously apparent.

The Introduction stressed that it lies in the very nature of an agreement providing for arms limitations that it could remain in force only as long as Russia, America and China each wanted to keep it in force. The agreement would not be weakened, but, rather, it would be strengthened, by giving these three nations and perhaps also certain other nations the legal right to abrogate the agreement at any time and without cause, because there would then be no need to spell out in the agreement specific measures of inspection. Instead, it would then be understood that if Russia, for instance, were unable to convince America that there were no major evasions on her territory, America would have no choice but to abrogate the agreement. The same would, of course, hold, in the reverse, for Russia.

With the problem presented in this manner, clearly the issue was no longer what rights of inspection America should demand from Russia or Russia should demand from America, but, rather, in what manner Russia might choose to convince America that there were no secret evasions on her territory, and in what manner America might choose to convince Russia.

At the outset of the meeting, the steering committee proposed that the simplest questions be discussed first; it proposed that the conference assume, for the sake of argument, an agreement providing for virtually complete disarmament, and that it discuss on this basis in what manner Russia and America could convince each other that they were not secretly evading the agreement.

In the course of the discussion, it became clear that in case of total disarmament, where there would be no military secrets left that would need to be safeguarded, the Russians would have no objection to admitting as many foreign inspectors as appeared desirable to America or any other nation. But thereupon most of the Americans took the position that by admitting foreign inspectors in practically unlimited numbers Russia could not convince them that she did not have hidden rockets or bombs in substantial numbers. If the Russian government wanted to hide bombs and rockets—so these Americans declared—as long as she had the wholehearted co-operation of her scientists and engineers in such an endeavor America could not be sure that foreign inspectors would be able to discover them.

At this point one of the Russian scientists proposed that, if and when general and total disarmament was agreed upon, Russia should reassure America on the issue of secret evasions by adopting the following approach: When the agreement was signed and published, the Chairman of the Council of Ministers would address the Russian people and, above all, the Russian engineers and scientists, over radio and television and through the newspapers. He would explain why the Russian government had entered into this agreement and why it wished to keep it in force. He would make it clear that any secret violation of the agreement would endanger the agreement and that the Russian government would not condone any such violation. If such violations did occur, as they well might, they would have to be regarded as the work of overzealous subordinates whose comprehension of Russia's true interests was rather limited. In these circumstances, it would be the patriotic duty of Russian citizens in general, and Russian scientists and engineers in particular, to report any secret violations of the agreement to an agent of the International Control Commission. In addition to having the satisfaction of fulfilling a patriotic duty, the informant would receive an award of $1 million from the Russian government.

A recipient of such an award who wished to enjoy his wealth by living a life of leisure and luxury abroad would be permitted to leave Russia with his family.

The Russian scientists pointed out that by repeating the same thesis over and over again, as they well knew how to do, the Russian government could create an atmosphere which would virtually guarantee that Russian scientists and engineers would come forward to report secret violations.

The Russians further proposed that agents of the International Control Commission maintain establishments in all Russian cities, and in the larger cities several establishments. An informant could simply walk into such an establishment with his whole family and make a deposition; if the International Control Commission held that the information revealed a violation of the agreement, then the Russian government would at once deposit the award of $1 million with the Commission. This sum would be returned to Russia if the information later turned out to be invalid, but the burden of proof would be on the Russian government.

The Russians thought that most Russian informants would probably prefer to remain in Russia. They proposed that such informants be free to remain, but that if they did they be required to report their whereabouts once every six months to the Control Commission, in order to satisfy the Commission that they had not been arrested or shot. Each time they reported they would receive an installment of their million-dollar award.

The Russians proposed that the arrest or shooting of an informant be classed as a violation of the disarmament agreement and that the reporting of this type of violation rate an award of $1 million, payable by the Russian government.

The response of the Americans to this novel Russian approach was very enthusiastic. The Americans said that they would favor America's adopting the same approach for reassuring Russia on possible secret violations. They said that the President would never condone such violations, but that the possibility of such violations could not be ruled out, since they might well be kept secret from the President. They also said that an award of $1 million would be almost meaningless in America, income tax being what it is, unless the Treasury issued a ruling that such awards would be free from tax. They did not doubt, however, that the Treasury could be prevailed upon to issue such a ruling.

The Americans also said they would recommend that every boat and plane capable of carrying a bomb across the Atlantic or the Pacific should carry a team of inspectors on board, in order to reassure Russia and China that these planes or ships did not carry any illicit bombs.

The discussion of safeguards in the case of virtually total disarmament ended with several Russian participants cautioning the conference against drawing the conclusion that satisfactory safeguards against secret violations would be practicable under prevailing world conditions. Since Russia would undoubtedly insist on retaining bombs and rockets for her defense—so they pointed out—and since these would be moved about on trucks and railroad cars, their current location would represent an important military secret that needed to be safeguarded. In these circumstances, clearly Russia would not be able to tolerate that the locations of the mobile rocket units be reported by informants.

The discussion of these arguments was deferred to the next series of sessions, which was supposed to examine the "feasibility" of controlled-arms reduction rather than virtually complete disarmament.

In preparation for that series of sessions, the steering committee drafted a memorandum, "Inspecting the Informant." This memorandum assumed that as a first step all submarines capable of firing rockets would be destroyed, and that at the

59

same time China, Russia and America would reduce the number of rockets below the shake-up level of the smaller nations. The number of bombs and rockets legitimately retained by America, China, Russia and the other nations would be agreed upon. The legitimately retained bombs and rockets would be marked and all the unmarked bombs and rockets retained would be considered illegitimate.

It was assumed that the legitimately retained rockets would be mounted on railroad cars or trucks and be constantly moved about. A sufficient number of rocket-tracing stations would be set up all over the world; these stations, by locating the origin of the rocket, would be capable of identifying the nation from whose territory the rocket was launched. It was proposed that each railroad car or truck carrying a legitimate rocket also carry an international team of inspectors. In case of an attack by a mobile-rocket unit which was not authorized by its government, the inspection teams would thus be in a position to exonerate the innocent units and to identify, by elimination, the particular one that had fired the rocket. The individuals responsible for such an unauthorized attack could then be brought to justice.

The teams of international inspectors assigned to the mobile rocket units would also serve as "markers," and any would-be informant could know that a unit not so marked was not a legitimate one.

It was made clear that in this stage of arms limitations there would be no secrets left that need be safeguarded, save the location of the mobile rocket units. Accordingly, informants would be free to transmit any information they pleased except this. In order to reassure the nations on this particular point, their governments would be permitted to "inspect" informants engaged in the process of transmitting information.

The memorandum stressed that even if the number of bombs and rockets which the nations were initially permitted to retain was very large, the further reduction of this number would be easy to police, because international inspectors could be called in to witness the destruction of each such bomb and rocket. How fast the initially retained number would be reduced would have to depend on the wishes of the participating nations. The reduction would have to take place step by step, and the magnitude of each step, as well as its timing, would have to be agreed upon from time to time.

Finally, the memorandum made it clear that controlled arms limitations of the kind envisaged would not greatly diminish the danger of clashes between the Great Powers, unless the acceptance of these limitations were accompanied by a determination and a pledge not to resort to atomic bombs except in retaliation against an attack with atomic bombs. If the nations were left free to bring pressure to bear on each other by threatening to use their legitimately retained bombs, then the limitation of the number of rockets would not appreciably diminish the danger of a resort to force.

During the discussion of this memorandum it became evident that some of the Americans were far from being reassured. They did not doubt that secret violations of the agreement would be detected if the approach proposed by the Russians were in fact adopted, but they were not sure that America would abrogate an agreement even if a rather serious violation were discovered. This provoked the Russians to say that they were prepared to deal with the difficulties that might arise from the distrust of the Russian government by the Americans, but were at a loss how to cope with problems arising from the fact that the Americans did not trust their own government.

Notwithstanding this first whimsical response, the Russians understood that the problem of abrogation was rather serious, and when the meeting reached an impasse on this subject they suggested that the steering committee prepare

61

a working paper on abrogations for the consideration of the conference. The paper which was prepared made two basic points:

1. The right to abrogate should be retained by only a small number of nations.
2. The nations retaining the right to abrogate must not be forced to choose between the two extremes of either tolerating serious violations of the agreement or invoking total abrogation of the agreement. These nations must be able to invoke a partial abrogation of the agreement, but might choose only a partial abrogation leading to one of the "balanced stages of reduced arms levels" specified in advance.

The working paper on abrogations proposed that the disarmament agreement specify a number of such predetermined "balanced stages of reduced arms levels," which were intermediate between the prevailing arms level and virtually total disarmament. It was assumed that the transition from a higher to a lower "balanced stage" would require a majority decision of the Security Council, with the concurring vote of the five permanent members. It was proposed that any permanent member of the Security Council should have the right to invoke either a limited or an all-out abrogation of the agreement and thereby to raise the arms level from the stage prevailing at the time of the abrogation to one of the higher of the ten stages specified in the agreement.

The working paper explained that an abrogation, or even a partial abrogation, of the agreement would have to be regarded as a matter of last resort and that it was essential to have the possibility of bringing other pressure on nations who violated the agreement. To this end, it was proposed that a certain sizable fraction of the amounts saved by the nations in arms cost be paid into a fund, the Fund for Compensations. If a nation that did not retain the right to abrogate were to violate the agreement, it could then be effectively restrained by economic sanctions, because the nations applying such sanctions could be, and would be, compensated for such economic losses as they themselves would suffer.

After an intermission of ten days, which the participants in the conference spent in the Semmering Mountains conversing with each other unencumbered by any agenda, the conference reconvened in Vienna. Because the existing political situation in Europe made the discussion of a political settlement appear to be purely academic, this part of the conference disappointed those who expected it to produce concrete suggestions in the domain of practical politics.

A Blue Book prepared by the steering committee was placed before the conference when it reconvened. It attributed the difficulties of Europe to the fact that the political structure in Europe did not reflect the economic interdependence of the nations of Europe, and it suggested that if Germany were not only economically but also politically integrated with Europe, Europe would pose no greater problem to the world than the other continents.

The steering committee took a dim view, however, of the possibility of bringing about political integration of Europe through the creation of supranational political agencies. Instead, it proposed a method of political integration which could be carried out gradually, step by step, and could start out, for instance, with the integration of France and Germany. As a first step, Germany would be represented in France, in the parliament of the Seventh Republic, by delegates who would have 5 per cent of the total votes. Similarly, France would be represented in the German parliament by delegates having 5 per cent of the total votes. In subsequent

63

years these representations could increase step by step, at a predetermined rate, until they might amount to 15 per cent of the votes in both parliaments.

In much the same manner, the committee thought, through mutual representation of the nations in each other's parliament the whole of Western Europe could be politically integrated.

This proposal encountered much skepticism at the conference. It was pointed out that while such a proposal might be received enthusiastically in France, it would have no chance of being passed by the German parliament. There it would be opposed by the People's Party, controlling 45 per cent of the votes, and would thus fall far short of the required two-thirds majority. Those who read the transcript of the conference may notice, in retrospect, that the Chinese and the Americans were much more vocal in expressing these misgivings than were the Russians. The Russians met several times among themselves and they must have discussed this problem, but they kept silent about it during the formal sessions.

The second part of the conference, having run out of topics that could be usefully discussed, closed one week earlier than scheduled.

Governmental negotiations on disarmament started about four months after the close of the Vienna Conference. They did not evoke much enthusiasm either in Russia or in America. The Americans were generally lukewarm and said that these negotiations could at best achieve arms reduction, which would not eliminate the possibility of war between the Great Powers; the Russians had misgivings that world public opinion might push them further toward total disarmament than they felt they ought to go.

The fears of the Russians proved to be groundless, inasmuch as the agreement closely paralleled the line that the

Russians had taken at the Vienna Conference. The agreement reduced the number of rockets and bombs to be retained by America, China and Russia below the shake-up level of the smaller nations, and it did eliminate all submarines capable of launching rockets; but it left Russia, America and China each in possession of one hundred long-range rockets capable of carrying 10-megaton clean hydrogen bombs. The agreement also fixed the number of rockets and bombs which the other nations were permitted to retain. All nations were pledged not to resort to the use of atomic bombs except in retaliation for an atomic-bomb attack.

As the result of the disarmament agreement, the nations were able to reduce their arms expenditure somewhat, but they were obliged to pay a good portion of what they saved in arms cost into the Fund for Compensation.

There was nothing in the agreement to offer any assurance that general and virtually complete disarmament would be achieved in the predictable future. True enough, the agreement defined the stages through which the world could go from the initial arms level (stage one) to virtually complete disarmament (stage ten). But the date of the transition from one stage to the next was left to the determination of the Security Council, where Russia had the veto, and there was no way of telling when, if ever, progress toward disarmament might take place.

Then, out of the blue, three months after the ratification of the agreement, Russia offered to cede to Poland each year, over a twenty-five-year period, strips of territory three to ten miles wide along Poland's eastern border, on condition that Poland cede year by year similar strips of territory on her western border to Germany. Poland declared herself willing to accept such a switch, but demanded a compensation of $25,000 for each Polish family which had to be relocated. This would have meant an outlay of $100 billion, payable

65

over a period of twenty-five years, or about $4 billion a year.

The Fund for Compensation would have been able to take on this load without too much difficulty, but this would have required approval by the Assembly and many nations were outraged by Poland's demand, which they regarded as extortion.

Still, in the end, the Assembly did approve; and since not even the Germans are prepared to go to war for something they can get without war, the approval of the Assembly split the People's Party in Germany. Half of its members seceded from the party and joined the other parties in voting for a constitutional amendment which provided for French representation in the German parliament, amounting initially to 5 per cent and after three years to 10 per cent of the total votes. As could be expected, France reciprocated.

With the adoption of this amendment the danger that the People's Party might gain a majority in the German parliament receded, and two years later the Security Council voted, with the five permanent members concurring, to reduce the arms level from stage one to stage four. Within five years the arms level was down to stage seven.

The disarmament agreement stipulated that mobile international armed forces, equipped with machine guns and light tanks of considerable fire power, be set up under United Nations auspices, but it did not say in what manner such forces would be controlled by the UN. In this respect the stipulation had been left vague on purpose, in order to secure acceptance of the agreement. During the negotiations the Russians had been pressing for the setting up of a world armed force under the central command of the United Nations, with the Secretary General being the commander in chief of the force. Since three of the previous Secretaries had had marked pro-Russian leanings, it is not surprising that America opposed a setup of this type. Most of the other nations rejected the setup proposed by America on the ground that it ran counter to sound principles of administration.

After the settlement of the German-Polish issue, negotiations on the setting up of some international armed force were reopened, and it was then agreed to set up a number of regional international armed forces under UN auspices rather than a single world armed force under the central command of the UN Secretariat. It was agreed that each such regional armed force should be under the control of five nations, who would appoint, by majority vote, the commander in chief. The slate of the five nations was to be subject to the approval of the UN Security Council, with the concurring vote of the five permanent members. One third of the cost of maintaining the regional force was to be borne by the five nations assuming the responsibility for maintaining peace in the region, and two thirds of the cost was to come from the Fund for Compensation.

This agreement did not appear to represent any real progress, because at first all slates proposed were vetoed by either Russia, China or America. One year later, however, when Russia and China proposed a slate of five nations for the control of a regional armed force for central Africa, where the expansionist tendencies of some of the new African nations represented a constant threat to their neighbors, unexpectedly America concurred and the slate was approved by the Security Council.*

---

* America, owing to the implacable hostility of the African political leaders toward her, had lost interest in Africa by 1987. This brought to an end a period of American-African relations which started in 1960, when the Kennedy Foundation allocated a modest sum to bring to the United States African students on American fellowships, and, on Vice-President Nixon's initiative, the State Department allocated a similar sum for the same purpose. From these modest beginnings there grew a vast fellowship program for Africans which brought over thousands of African stu-

The decision of the Soviet Union to concur in the reduction of the arms level from stage one to stage four followed, within a month, the establishment of the regional armed force for central Africa. The subsequent reduction of the arms level from stage four to stage seven followed the establishment of regional armed forces in the Middle East, in Southeast Asia and in Central America.

The drastic reduction of the arms level to stage seven resulted for many countries in a considerable saving in arms cost. This did not amount to very much in the case of Russia, since she had based her defense almost exclusively on long-range rockets, but it was very substantial in the case of America. It had always been taken for granted that when disarmament made a substantial reduction in arms cost possible there would be a great increase in aid to underdeveloped countries. What happened was the opposite. Americans felt that, after a long period of stagnation, the time had come to increase the standard of living. There was a substantial reduction in taxes, and wages went up. The annual income of the average American family jumped by about $2,000. In the first five years following ratification of the disarmament agreement, Congress failed to appropriate any funds for foreign aid. A modest Point Four program was retained, but it did not amount to very much, because, high-school education having steadily deteriorated in America, she was in no position to send a substantial number of engineers and physicians abroad.

Russia had retained the six-day work week, but had in-

---

dents every year to America, where they received a college education. From among their ranks came most of Africa's political leaders. Their subsequent hostility to America is rather puzzling, because even though they may have been exposed to a certain amount of racial discrimination while studying in America, they could not have been any worse off, in this respect, than the American-born colored citizens of the United States.

creased the annual paid vacation to three months and was in the process of trying to extend the vacation period to four months. Russia continued to lend funds to underdeveloped nations even after the conclusion of the disarmament agreement, but she charged 5 per cent on such loans. Russia also continued to make available to underdeveloped nations the services of her engineers and physicians, and this was being done on a large scale, but after the conclusion of the disarmament agreement she began to charge for these services, whatever the market would bear.

While the events of the decades that followed general disarmament are of great historical interest, they do not come within the scope of this dissertation. My task here is to appraise the contribution that the dolphins made toward the establishment of lasting peace, and the dolphins faded out of the picture soon after general disarmament had been attained.

A week after the arms level was reduced to stage seven, a virus epidemic broke out among the dolphins at the Vienna Institute and one dolphin after another died. Two weeks after the death of the last dolphin, a fire broke out in the library of the Institute, which destroyed most of the books and, with a very few exceptions, all of the records. Thereafter, the Russians and the Americans who composed the staff of the Institute decided to abandon Vienna and to return to their homelands.

The decision to disband the laboratories of the Vienna Institute was regarded as a major blow to science and was greatly deplored all over the world. The Russian and American scientists who returned home were able to continue their work in the Crimea and in California respectively, where new research institutes were set up to accommodate them. In the years that followed these institutes turned out work which was in no way inferior to the work of the Vienna Institute

69

`but neither the Russian nor the American scientists attempted again to communicate with dolphins. No other international research project was set up to emulate the work of the Vienna Institute with dolphins, even though suggestions to set up such a project on a broader international basis were made by the British, French, Italian and Chinese governments. The German government established a very large research operation in Munich on a purely national basis, with the aim of continuing the work of the Vienna Institute with dolphins. The Munich Institute was staffed entirely with German biologists, and inasmuch as the funds were provided by the German government alone, it was deemed proper that the results of the work should benefit Germany only. The director of the Munich Institute announced at the outset that the results of experiments initiated by the staff themselves would be published, but that experiments undertaken on the advice of the dolphins and information relating to the dolphins themselves would come under the Official Secrets Act.

From the very first year of its existence, the Munich Institute published papers on a great variety of scientific subjects, many of them rather voluminous. All of them were published under the name of the scientists who performed the experiments, and no credit was given to any dolphin. While all of this work was respectable and some of it quite informative, none of it was extraordinary.

In the Munich Institute's fifth year of operation, one of the members of the staff was sued for divorce by his wife. During the ensuing court wrangle, which was exceedingly bitter, the wife testified that, in addition to his salary from the Institute, her husband derived about an equal amount of income as a consultant to industrial corporations. She said, on the witness stand, that in the Institute's third year there had been some talk that its director might resign, that the Institute might be dissolved and that the staff might be transferred to various research institutions in Frankfurt, Göttingen, Cologne or Leipzig, all of which were much less pleasant places to live than Munich. At that time there were rumors that the staff had found it impossible to learn the language of the dolphins, that they came to doubt that the dolphins had a language that could be learned, and that all of the experiments carried out by the staff represented the efforts of the staff themselves.

These proceedings in court attracted considerable attention in Munich, where it had been noted previously that the staff of the Institute appeared to live above their means. The U.S. Senate Committee on Internal Security also got into the act, and it subpoenaed several of the former staff members of the Vienna Institute who had returned to America. A minor stir was created when all of these men refused to testify, but since they were not suspected of being Communists there was no attempt to cite them for contempt. Some columnists chided the scientists and sided with the Congressional committee, but most of the others stressed that refusing to testify could in no way be construed as an admission of guilt.

There were, of course, those who questioned whether the Vienna Institute had in fact been able to communicate with dolphins and whether the dolphins were in any way responsible for the conspicuous achievements of the Vienna Institute. America being a free country, any one can think and say, of course, what he pleases. It is difficult to see, however, how the Vienna Institute could have accomplished as much as it did if it hadn't been able to draw on considerably more than the knowledge and wisdom of the Russian and American scientists who composed its staff.

[1960]

71

My Trial as a War Criminal

My Trial as a War Criminal

I WAS JUST ABOUT to lock the door of my hotel room and go to bed when there was a knock on the door and there stood a Russian officer and a young Russian civilian. I had expected something of this sort ever since the President signed the terms of unconditional surrender and the Russians landed a token occupation force in New York. The officer handed me something that looked like a warrant and said that I was under arrest as a war criminal on the basis of my activities during the Second World War in connection with the atomic bomb. There was a car waiting outside and they told me that they were going to take me to the Brookhaven National Laboratory on Long Island. Apparently, they were rounding up all the scientists who had ever worked in the field of atomic energy.

Once we were in the car the young man introduced himself and told me that he was a physicist as well as a member of the Moscow Chapter of the Communist Party. I had never heard his name before and I was never able to remember it thereafter. He was obviously very eager to talk. He told me that he and the other Russian scientists were all exceedingly sorry that the strain of the virus which had been used had killed such a disproportionately large number of children. It was very fortunate, he said, that the first attack was limited to New Jersey and that the early cessation of hostilities made attacks of larger scope unnecessary. According to plan—so he said—stocks of this virus were merely held in reserve for an emergency. Another virus differing by five further mutational steps had been in the stage of pilot plant production, and it was this improved virus which was meant to be used in case of war. It would not affect children at all and would kill predominantly men between twenty and forty. Owing to the premature outbreak of the war, however, the Russian government found itself forced to use the stocks which it had on hand.

He said that all the scientists arrested would be given a chance to go to Russia, in which case they need not stand trial as war criminals; but that if I should elect to stand for trial he personally hoped that I would be exonerated and that afterward I would be willing to collaborate with the Russians here in the United States.

He said that the Russians were very anxious to get the support of people other than the American Communists for a stable political regime in the United States which would collaborate with them. Since they now had the support of the

Communists anyway, he explained, they would rather bestow their favors on those whose co-operation was not yet assured. "We shall, of course, lean on the Communists for the next few months," he said, "but, in the long run, dissatisfied elements who are used to conspiracy would not be relied on by us. It is difficult to work with fellows who have no sense of humor," he added as an afterthought.

He told me that no scientist would be forced to go to Russia and that no one who was innocent need go there for fear of having to stand trial as a war criminal, because, he said, Russia would do everything in her power to make the trials fair and impartial. "The outcome of a bona fide trial," he added somewhat illogically, "is, of course, always something of a tossup."

He told me that he expected that Russia would, within a fortnight, change her position on the question of world government; that she would come out in favor of it, in principle, and that she would press for immediate strengthening of the United Nations. The tribunal which was being assembled to try war criminals would not be Russian-dominated, he said, but would, rather, be composed of representatives of all nations which were not at war with Russia.

I was surprised to hear him say that he expected Great Britain to delegate the Lord Chief Justice to sit on the tribunal, and, frankly, I did not believe him then, though of course this was technically not impossible, since the coalition Cabinet had declared Britain's neutrality twenty-four hours before the outbreak of the war. His prediction was confirmed, however, the following morning when the newspapers reported the speech of the British Prime Minister, who had said that Great Britain, having participated in the Nuremberg trials, could not now refuse her participation without being guilty of displaying a double standard of morality. The information which I received from this young man proved to be most

77

valuable to me, because it gave me time to make up my mind as to what line I would want to follow.

As far as going to Russia was concerned, my mind was made up. After having been raised in Hungary, I had lived in Germany and in England before I settled in the United States, and that is as much migration as is good for any man. Moreover, when you are above fifty you are no longer as quick at learning languages. How many years would it take me to get a sufficient command of Russian to be able to turn a phrase and to be slightly malicious without being outright offensive? No, I did not want to go to Russia.

Even less did I want to be put in the position of having favors bestowed upon me by the Russians or of having to refuse point-blank some position of importance which they might wish to offer to me. I did not want to incur the favor of the Russians, but I did not want to antagonize them, either. After devoting some thought to this dilemma, I decided that the best way for me to keep out of trouble was to stick to the truth and thereby to arouse the suspicion of the Russians.

I did not have to wait long for an opportunity to implement this plan of action. The next morning at Brookhaven I was interrogated by a Russian official. In the beginning his attitude was rather benevolent. Almost the first question he asked me was why I had not worked in the field of atomic energy prior to the Third World War. When I truthfully said that I had five good and valid reasons and named them one by one, he took them down in shorthand, but the longer I talked the more incredulous he looked. It was obvious that he felt himself unable to believe what I was saying to him. Realizing that my method worked, I answered all his questions as truthfully as I possibly could and then signed the transcript at the end of the interview.

I was called back for further interrogation in the afternoon; this time it was an older Russian scientist, who was known to

78

me by name, but whom I had not previously met. He told me
that he had asked to see me because he had read the transcript which I had signed in the morning. He said that the
Russian scientists had followed with great interest the articles
I had written before the war, and he quoted to me passages
from articles entitled "Calling for a Crusade" and "Letter to
Stalin" which I had published in the *Bulletin of the Atomic
Scientists* in 1947. This pleased me very much. He went on to
say, however, that these articles showed an almost incredible
degree of naïveté and were models of un-Marxian writing. He
acknowledged that they were free from any anti-Russian bias
and told me that the Russian scientists had formed the opinion that I had not been working in the field of atomic energy
before the Third World War because I had not wanted to
make bombs that would be dropped on Russia. He said that
he regretted that I had not given this as my reason, that he
wanted to give me an opportunity to revise the answers which
I had given, and that he was prepared to tear up my signed
statement then and there, though by doing so he would be
sticking his neck out, since he would be acting against regula-
tions.

I thanked him for his kindness and told him that I had
merely told the truth, which, unfortunately, it was not within
my power to change; and there then ensued a most interesting and protracted conversation about the intrinsic value of
truth. Since what he told me was told in confidence and
might get him into trouble if revealed, I do not feel free to
record it here.

The war crimes trials opened about one month later at
Lake Success, and I was—apparently as a special favor—
among the first to be tried. I was charged by the prosecutor,
a Russian, first of all with having tried to induce the United
States government to take up the development of atomic
energy in a meeting held on October 21, 1939, i.e., at a time

when the war in Europe was still an imperialist war, since Germany had not attacked Russia until 1941.

I was also charged with having contributed to the war crime of dropping an atomic bomb on Hiroshima. I thought at first that I had a good and valid defense against this latter charge, since I had warned against the military use of the bomb in the war with Japan in a memorandum which I had presented to Mr. Byrnes at Spartanburg, South Carolina, six weeks before the first bomb had been tested in New Mexico.

But unfortunately this memorandum, which Mr. Byrnes had put into a pocket of his trousers when I left him, could not be located by counsel for the defense either in the files of the State Department or in the possession of any of the Spartanburg cleaners who might have kept it as a souvenir. Mr. Byrnes was himself under indictment and was not called as a witness. Excerpts from the memorandum which were published in the fall of 1947 in the *Bulletin of the Atomic Scientists* were stricken from the record on the ground that the parts of this memorandum which were omitted from the publication for reasons of secrecy might have contained the opposite of what the published part of the document appeared to indicate.

Under these circumstances I had to fall back for my defense on a petition which I had circulated in the Uranium Project at the University of Chicago immediately after the testing of the bomb in New Mexico and which asked the President to withhold his approval of a military use of the bomb against the cities of Japan. The prosecutor moved, however, that this document be stricken from the record on the ground that it was not transmitted by me to the President directly, but was, rather, handed by me to the head of the project, who forwarded it through the Manhattan District of the War Department, headed by General Groves. The prosecutor said that I, Szilard, should have known better than to agree to such a method of transmittal.

Having rested my defense, I was now free on bail. Since I was not permitted to leave Lake Success, I was spending my time there listening to the trials of the statesmen and scientists. In spite of the seriousness of my own situation, I found it difficult sometimes to refrain from joining in the laughter which frequently interrupted the proceedings.

As a prelude to the Nuremberg trials, war crimes had been defined with the collaboration of the United States, represented by Justice Jackson of the United States Supreme Court. The "violation of the customs of war" had been defined as a war crime at that time. "Planning a war in violation of international agreements" had also been defined as a crime.

The first statesman to be tried on charges arising from the bombing of Hiroshima was Mr. Stimson, and he was tried on his own admission contained in an article which he had published in 1947 in *Harper's*. The prosecution pointed out that the "defense" put forward by Mr. Stimson in that article was untenable. Mr. Stimson's point was that, had the bomb not been used, millions would have perished in an invasion of Japan. The prosecutor, a Dutchman, quoted from a memorandum prepared after the surrender of Japan by the United States Strategic Bombing Survey which showed that the United States could have won the war against Japan without invasion, just by sitting tight, since Japan was essentially defeated before the bomb was dropped on Hiroshima. He further quoted passages from the book *Secret Mission*, by Ellis M. Zacharias, published in 1946, which showed that Japan's desperate position must have been known to Mr. Stimson, since it was fully disclosed in the reports prepared by the United States naval intelligence.

Counsel for the Defense, however, submitted a deposition

81

obtained from the British Secretary of War in order to prove that secretaries of war never based decisions on reports prepared by naval intelligence. "Mr. Stimson," so counsel for the defense said, "should not be reproached for acting as all secretaries of war in all English-speaking countries have acted at all times."

The presiding judge, in summing up, disregarded the arguments presented by both the prosecution and the defense and took the line that prior to the Third World War it was not customary to drop atomic bombs on towns and cities, and that such a "violation of the customs of war" was a war crime which could not be justified on the ground that the government which committed it hoped that by doing so it would bring the war to a speedier conclusion.

It was expected that Mr. Stimson would be found guilty on his own admission, but that he would be reprieved primarily because of his article published in *Foreign Affairs* in 1947 in which he commented on the foreign policy of the Truman Administration. It was generally considered that in 1947 his was a voice of reason and moderation in the midst of general confusion.

Mr. Truman was charged with the "crime" of actually ordering the bombing of Hiroshima. At first, counsel for the defense took the line that at the time when the definition of war crimes was made public at Nuremberg, Mr. Truman was at sea—in the literal sense of the term. He was on board a battleship on his way back from Potsdam and did not have opportunity adequately to study the text of the Nuremberg Declaration prior to the bombing of Hiroshima. This plea was rejected by the court on the ground that those who were sentenced to death and executed at Nuremberg could—if they were alive—use much the same type of argument in their defense.

Subsequently, counsel for the defense took the line that Mr. Truman was not guilty because he had not acted on his own but had merely followed advice given to him and, so to speak, had been merely following orders. In proof of this the defense read into the record a magazine article published by Garbatov in Russia in 1947 which asserted that Mr. Truman had always been taking orders from one boss or another. This article had drawn a protest from the American ambassador at the time of its publication.

Having had little luck with any of his "lines," counsel for the defense raised the question why the use of an atomic bomb should be considered a "violation of the customs of war" any more than the use of a virus that killed children. But the presiding judge ordered his remark stricken from the record, saying that this was the trial of Harry S. Truman and not of Somebody Else, and that since Mr. Truman was not accused of having ordered the use of a virus in warfare, nothing relating to any virus could possibly be relevant to his defense.

It was generally expected that Mr. Truman would be found guilty, but it was rumored that there were powerful Russian influences at work to have him reprieved. There were all sorts of guesses as to what the reasons of the Russians may have been, and some thought that they favored Mr. Truman on account of his supposed Wall Street connections, since the Russians were known to nurture a secret admiration for Wall Street. I, myself, believe that the reason of the Russians may have been political and rather difficult to guess in detail without knowing on which of their misconceptions it was based.

The next to be tried was Mr. Byrnes, who was not only accused of being responsible for the decision of using the atomic bomb against Japan, but, above all, was accused of having advocated a war against Russia "in violation of inter-

83

national agreements" in his book *Speaking Frankly*, which appeared in 1947. The British prosecutor quoted from page 203 of the first edition:

> . . . I do not believe the Red Army would try to hold permanently all of Eastern Germany. However, if I misjudge them, and they do go to the point of holding Eastern Germany and vetoing a Security Council Directive to withdraw occupation forces, we must be prepared to assume the obligation that then clearly will be ours. If our action is to be effective, we must be clear in our minds and must make it clear to all that we are willing to adopt these measures of last resort if, for the peace of the world, we are forced to do so.

On this passage Mr. Byrnes was most severely cross-examined by the prosecutor. He was asked whether he was aware of the fact that the United States ratified the Charter of the United Nations at the time when Mr. Byrnes himself was Secretary of State. He was asked whether he was aware of the fact that by doing so the United States undertook the solemn obligation of refraining from war and that, under Article 51 of the Charter, the United States merely retained the right of waging war in case of an armed attack. He was asked whether the mere refusal of Russia to leave the territories which she had occupied after the Second World War could be construed as an armed attack. He was asked whether he could suggest any way of interpreting what he had been saying on page 203 of his book other than as advocating that the United States ought to violate her solemn obligation under the Charter and wage an illegal war against Russia in case Russia should refuse to settle on the terms set by the United States government.

Counsel for the defense replied that he wished to elucidate the meaning of the passage "measures of last resort" quoted by the prosecutor from Mr. Byrnes's book. At a press conference following shortly the publication of his book, Mr. Byrnes himself had explained this passage—so counsel for the defense said. " 'There is no suggestion as to whether such collective action should be persuasion, economic, or military action,' " counsel quoted. "Clearly," counsel said, raising his voice a little, "if Mr. Byrnes had had *military action* in mind, he would have spoken of 'measures of very last resort' and not merely of 'measures of last resort.' British statesmen," he said, looking sharply at the prosecutor, "may indulge in understatements, but that is no reason for accusing my client of one."

The prosecutor replied that Mr. Byrnes had condemned himself by the very words quoted by the defense, for by virtue of those words Mr. Byrnes had admitted that the term "measures of last resort" meant either persuasion or military action. "I am not conversant with American law," he said, "but surely in England a man who publicly proclaims that he is going to get hold of something that is in the possession of his neighbor either by persuasion or by pulling a gun on him is persuaded to go to jail."

At this point, counsel for the defense submitted evidence to show that, two weeks before the outbreak of the Third World War, Mr. Byrnes had sent a memorandum to the President of the United States warning against any aggressive act on the part of the United States armed forces that would result in war. The prosecutor's motion that this memorandum be ruled out as evidence was upheld by the presiding judge on the ground that if inconsistency were admissible as a defense at the trial of a statesman, then no statesman could ever be convicted as a war criminal and the statesmen would enjoy an immunity not shared by the other defendants.

All of us who attended his trial were unanimous in our praise of Mr. Byrnes for the patience and firmness he displayed. Of course, if sentence had been passed and executed, he would have lost his life; but as is generally known, no sentence was ever passed on Mr. Byrnes or any of the rest of us. The first Russian appeal for help reached the United States Public Health Service one week after Mr. Byrnes rested his defense.

Just what happened will never be known with certainty. This much is clear, that the vast quantities of vaccine which the Russians held in readiness to safeguard their own population against the virus were absolutely without any effect. In the laboratory tests such vaccine had proved to be 100 per cent effective; something must have gone wrong in the change-over from pilot plant operation to mass production, and someone must have forgotten to check the product for its effectiveness. Since the engineer in charge of the production plant at Omsk perished in the disorders which broke out after over half of the children of the town had died, and since all records of the production plants were destroyed in the fire, we shall never know just what had gone wrong.

The terms of the postwar settlement which had been reached within two weeks of the Omsk riots were in every respect very favorable to the United States and also put an end to all war crime trials. Naturally, all of us who had been on trial for our lives were greatly relieved.

[1947]

The Mark Gable Foundation

The Mark Gable Foundation

As soon as I saw the temperature of the rabbit come back to normal, I knew that we had licked the problem. It took twenty-four hours to bring his temperature down to one degree centigrade, injecting three grains of dorminol every ten minutes during that period. Sleep set in between the third and fourth hours, when the body temperature fell below twenty-six centigrade; and after twenty-four hours, at one centigrade, there was no longer any appreciable metabolic activity. We kept him at that low temperature for one day, after which time, having completed our measurements, we injected metaboline and allowed the temperature to rise to normal within one hour.

There was never any doubt in my mind that once we got this far, and got the temperature down to one centigrade, we could keep the rabbit "asleep" for a week, a year or a hundred years just as well as for a day. Nor had I much doubt that if this worked for the rabbit it would work for the dog; and that if it worked for the dog, it would work for man.

I always wanted to see what kind of place the world will be three hundred years hence. I intended to "withdraw from life" (as we proposed to call the process) as soon as we had perfected the method, and to arrange for being returned to life in 2260. I thought my views and sentiments were sufficiently advanced, and that I had no reason to fear I should be too much behind the times in a world that had advanced a few hundred years beyond the present. I would not have dared, though, to go much beyond three hundred years.

I thought at first that one year should be plenty for perfecting the process as well as for completing the arrangements; and that I should be *in statu dormiendi* before the year was over. As a matter of fact, it took only six months to get ready; but difficulties of an unforeseen kind arose.

A section of public opinion was strongly opposed to "withdrawal from life," and for a time it looked as though the Eighty-sixth Congress would pass a law against it. This, fortunately, did not come to pass. The A.M.A., however, succeeded in obtaining a court injunction against my "withdrawal" on the basis that it was "suicide," and suicide was unlawful. Since a man *in statu dormiendi* cannot of his own volition return to life—so the brief argued—from the legal point of view he is not living while in that state.

The ensuing legal battle lasted for five years. Finally Adams, Lynch and Davenport, who handled my case, succeeded in getting the Supreme Court to accept jurisdiction.

The Supreme Court upheld the injunction, with three justices dissenting. Mr. Davenport explained to me that the ruling of the Supreme Court, though on the face of it unfavorable, was in reality a very fortunate thing for me because it removed all obstacles that might have stood in the way of my plans. The ruling of the Supreme Court, Mr. Davenport explained, established once and for all that a man is not legally living while *in statu dormiendi*. Therefore, he said, if I should now decide to act against the advice of his firm, disregard the court injunction and proceed to withdraw from life, no legal action could be taken against me under any statute until I was returned to life three hundred years hence, at which time my offense would come under the statute of limitations.

All arrangements having been completed in secrecy, and having named Adams, Lynch and Davenport as executors of my estate, I spent my last evening in the twentieth century at a small farewell party given to me by friends. There were about six of us, all old friends, but somehow we did not understand each other very well on this occasion. Most of them seemed to have the feeling that they were sort of attending my funeral, since they would not see me again alive; whereas to me it seemed that it was I who was attending their funeral, since none of them would be alive when I woke up.

According to the records, it took about two hours until sleep set in, but I do not remember anything that was said after the first hour.

The next thing I remember was the prick of a needle, and when I opened my eyes I saw a nurse with a hypodermic syringe in one hand and a microphone in the other.

"Would you mind speaking into the microphone, please?" she said, holding it at a comfortable distance from my face.

"We owe you an apology, as well as an explanation," said a well-dressed young man standing near my bed and holding a microphone in his hand. "I am Mr. Rosenblatt from Adams, Lynch, Davenport, Rosenblatt and Giannini. For reasons of a legal nature we deemed it advisable to return you to life, but if you wish to complete the three hundred years, which appears to be your goal, we hope we shall be able to make the necessary arrangements within one month. At least we shall try our best to do so.

"Now, before you say anything, let me explain to you that the gentleman sitting next to me is Mr. McClintock, the mayor of the city—a Democrat, of course. Subject to your approval, we have agreed that he may give you an interview which will be televised. The proceeds will go to the Senile Degeneration Research Fund. The broadcasting companies understand, of course, that it's up to you to agree to this arrangement, and they have an alternate program ready which can be substituted if you should object. If you agree, however, we shall go on the air in one minute. Naturally, the broadcasting companies are anxious to catch your first responses rather than have something rehearsed put on the air. I'm certain you'll appreciate their point of view."

"Before I answer this," I said, "would you mind telling me how long I've been asleep?"

"I should have told you this before," he said. "You were out ninety years."

"Then," I said after a moment's reflection, "I have no friends left from whom to keep any secrets. I have no objection to the broadcast."

As soon as the announcer finished with his somewhat lengthy introduction, the mayor came in. "As chairman of the Senile Degeneration Research Fund, I wish to express my thanks to you for having graciously consented to this interview. Senile degeneration is one of our most important diseases. One in eight die of senile degeneration, and more than half of those who reach the age of a hundred and five. Given ample funds for research, we cannot fail to discover the causes of this disease, and once the cause of the disease is known it will be possible to find a cure. But I know that I should not monopolize the air; there must be many things that you would want to know about our society. Please feel free to ask anything you like."

"Why was I returned to life?" I asked.

"I'm certain," the mayor said, "that Messrs. Adams, Lynch, Davenport, Rosenblatt and Giannini will want to give you a detailed explanation of that. It was their decision, and I have no doubt that it was a wise one in the circumstances. I'm not a lawyer, but I can tell you something about the political background of their decision. Politics—that's my field.

"I wonder whether you realize how much trouble your process of 'withdrawal from life' has caused the government. For a few years only a few persons followed your example, mostly political scientists and anthropologists. But then, all of a sudden, it became quite a fad. People withdrew just to spite their wives and husbands. And I regret to say that many Catholics who could not obtain a divorce chose this method of surviving their husbands or wives, to become widowed and to remarry, until this practice was finally stopped in 2001 by the papal bull 'Somnus Naturae Repugnans.'

"The Church did not interfere, of course, with the legitimate uses of the process. Throughout the latter part of the century doctors encouraged patients who suffered from cancer and certain other incurable diseases to withdraw from life, in the hope that a cure would be found in the years to come and that they could then be returned to life and cured. There were legal complications, of course, particularly in the case of wealthy patients. Often their heirs raised objections on the ground that withdrawal from life was not yet an entirely safe process; and equally often the heirs demanded that they too should be permitted to withdraw from life for an equal period

93

of time, so that the natural sequence of the generations would be left undisturbed. There are about one million cancer patients at present *in statu dormiendi*, and half a million of their heirs."

"Then cancer is still not a curable disease?" I asked.

"No," the mayor said, "but with all the funds which are now available it can take at the most a few years until that problem is solved. The most important, even though a somewhat controversial, application of your process," he continued, "came about twenty-five years ago. That was when the present great depression started. It came as a result of seventy-five years of Republican mismanagement. Today we have a Democratic President and a Democratic Congress; but this is the first Democratic President since Donovan, and the first Democratic Congress since the Hundred and Fifth. As more and more of the Southern states began to vote Republican, our party was hopelessly outvoted, until gradually its voting strength began to rise again; and today, with a Democratic majority solidly established, we have nothing to fear from coming elections."

"So finally there's a truly progressive party in the United States?" I asked.

"Yes," the mayor said, "we regard ourselves as progressives. We have the support of the Catholic Church, and eighty per cent of the voters are Catholics."

"What brought about such mass conversions?" I asked.

"There were no mass conversions," the mayor said, "and we wouldn't want any. Families of Polish, Irish and Italian stock, having a stronger belief in the American way of life than some of the older immigrant stocks, have always given birth to more children; and so today we have a solid Catholic majority.

"Now that the Democratic Party is established in office,

94

we're going to fight the depression by the proper economic methods. As I said before, there was a Republican Administration in office when the depression hit us twenty-five years ago. In the first year of that depression unemployment rose to ten million. Things looked pretty bad. There was no public-works program or unemployment relief, but Congress passed a law, the Withdrawal Act of 2025, authorizing the use of Federal funds to enable any unemployed who so desired to withdraw from life for the duration of the depression. Those unemployed who availed themselves of this offer had to authorize the government to return them to life when the government deemed that the labor market required such a measure.

"Seven out of ten million unemployed availed themselves of this offer by the end of the first year, in spite of the opposition of the Church. The next year unemployment was up another seven million, out of which five million were withdrawn from life. This went on and on, and by the time our party got into office, two years ago, there were twenty-five million withdrawn from life, with Federal support.

"Our first act in office was to make withdrawals from life unlawful; and the second was to institute a public-works program."

"What does your public-works program consist of?" I asked.

"Housing," the mayor said.

"Is there a housing shortage?" I asked. "No," the mayor said. "With twenty-five million unemployed *in statu dormiendi* there is, of course, no housing shortage."

"And will you now return these twenty-five million unemployed to life?" I asked.

"Only very gradually," the mayor replied. "The majority of the sleepers are non-Catholics and it would upset the political balance if they were returned to life all at once.

95

Besides, operating the refrigerator plants of the public dormitories for twenty-five million sleepers is part of our public-works program.

"Incidentally," he added, "whether you yourself come under the Antiwithdrawal Act of 2048 is a controversial question. Your lawyers felt that you would not want to violate the law of the land, and they tried to get a court ruling in order to clear you; but the court refused to take the case, because you weren't legally alive; finally your lawyers decided to return you to life so that you may ask the court for a declaratory judgment. Even though there is little doubt that the court will rule in your favor, I personally hope that you'll find our society so pleasant, and so much more advanced than you would have expected, that you'll decide to stay with us in the twenty-first century."

"Thank you very much, Mr. Mayor," the announcer said. "This was beautiful timing. We're off the air," he said to me, thinking I needed more explanation.

The mayor turned to me. "If you feel well enough, I would like to take you home for dinner. It's a small party, four or five guests, my wife and my daughter Betty. The poor girl is brokenhearted. She has just called off her engagement, and I'm doing what I can to cheer her up. She's very much in love with the fellow."

"If she loves him so much, why did she break with him?" I asked.

"All her friends teased her about him because he wears teeth," the mayor said. "Of course, there's no law against it, it's just not done, that's all."

Something began to dawn upon me at this moment. The nurse, a pretty young girl, had no teeth, Mr. Rosenblatt had no teeth, and the mayor had no teeth. Teeth seemed to be out of fashion.

"I have teeth," I said.

96

"Yes, of course," the mayor replied, "and you wear them with dignity. But if you should decide to stay with us you'll want to get rid of them. They're not hygienic."

"But how would I chew my food, how do you chew your food?" I asked.

"Well," the mayor said, "we don't eat with our hands. We eat from plates—chewing plates. "They plug into sockets in the table and chew your food for you. We eat with spoons."

"Steaks, too?" I asked.

"Yes, everything," the mayor said. "But have no fear, we shall have knife and fork for you tonight, and flat plates such as you are accustomed to. My daughter kept them for her fiancé."

"I'm sorry that my second daughter will not be with us tonight," the mayor said as he was starting his car. "She's in the hospital. In college she's taking mathematics and chemistry. She could have talked to you in your own language."

"Nothing seriously wrong, I hope," I said.

"Oh, no!" the mayor said. "Just plastic surgery. She'll be out in a day or two."

"With a new nose?" I asked.

"Nothing wrong with her nose," the mayor said. "As a matter of fact, she has Mark Gable's nose. No, it's one of these newfangled operations. My wife and I don't approve of it, but this girl, she runs with the smart set. 'Esophagus bypass,' they call it. No longer necessary to watch your diet, you know. Eat as much as you please and switch it to the by-pass—goes into a rubber container, of course. I tried to talk her out of it, but that girl has an answer for everything. 'Father,' she said, isn't there a food surplus in the world? If everybody ate twice as much, would that not solve the problem?"

"Maybe she's right," I said, remembering with an effort that I always used to side with youth.

When we sat down at table I looked forward to the steak; I was pretty hungry by that time. But when it was served, after a few fruitless attempts with knife and fork I had to ask for a chewing plate.

"The choice cuts are always especially tough," my hostess explained.

"Tell me," I said, "when did people begin to discard their teeth, and why?"

"Well," the mayor said, "it started thirty years ago. Ford's chewing plates have been advertised over television for at least thirty-five years. Once people have chewing plates, what use do they have for teeth? If you think of all the time people used to spend at the dentist's, and for no good purpose, at that, you'll have to admit we have made progress."

"What became of all the dentists?" I asked.

"Many of them have been absorbed by the chewing-plate industry," the mayor explained, "Henry Ford VI gave them preference over all categories of skilled workers. Others turned to other occupations. Take Mr. Mark Gable, for instance," the mayor said, pointing to a man sitting at my right, a man about fifty, and of great personal charm. "He had studied dentistry; today he is one of the most popular donors, and the richest man in the United States."

"Oh," I said. "What is his business?"

"Over one million boys and girls," the mayor said "are his offspring in the United States, and the demand is still increasing."

"That must keep you pretty busy, Mr. Gable," I said, unable to think of anything else to say.

Apparently I had put my foot in it. Mrs. Gable blushed, and the mayor laughed.

98

"Mr. Gable is happily married," the mayor said. "He donated the seed when he was twenty-four years old. The stock should last indefinitely, although the demand may not. The Surgeon General has ruled that no seed donated by anyone above twenty-five may be marketed in the United States."

"Has there been legislation about this, giving the Surgeon General such authority?" I asked.

"No," the mayor said. "Legislation was blocked by filibuster in the Senate. But the Surgeon General takes action under the Pure Food and Drug Act."

"How can he do that?" I asked.

"There was a decision by the Supreme Court thirty years ago," the mayor said, "that all ponderable substance which is destined to enter through any orifice of the human body comes properly under that act. There was no legislation in this whole field whatsoever. Any woman who wishes to bear a child of her own husband is perfectly free to do so. Over fifteen per cent of the children are born in this manner; but most wives prefer to select a donor."

"How do they make a choice?" I asked.

"Oh," the mayor said, "the magazines are full of their pictures. You can see them on the screen at home and in the movies. There are fashions, of course. Today over seventy per cent of the 'donated' children are the offspring of the thirty-five most popular donors. Naturally, they're expensive. Today a seed of Mr. Gable's will bring a thousand dollars; but you can get seed from very good stock for a hundred. Fashions are bound to change, but long after Mr. Gable passes away his estate will still go on selling his seed to connoisseurs. It's estimated that for several decades his estate will still take in more than thirty million dollars a year."

"I have earned a very large sum of money," said Mr. Gable, turning to me, "with very little work. And now I'm thinking of setting up a trust fund. I want to do something that will

99

really contribute to the happiness of mankind; but it's very difficult to know what to do with money. When Mr. Rosenblatt told me that you'd be here tonight I asked the mayor to invite me. I certainly would value your advice."

"Would you intend to do anything for the advancement of science?" I asked.

"No," Mark Gable said. "I believe scientific progress is too fast as it is."

"I share your feeling about this point," I said with the fervor of conviction, "but then why not do something about the retardation of scientific progress?"

"That I would very much like to do," Mark Gable said, "but how do I go about it?"

"Well," I said, "I think that shouldn't be very difficult. As a matter of fact, I think it would be quite easy. You could set up a foundation, with an annual endowment of thirty million dollars. Research workers in need of funds could apply for grants, if they could make out a convincing case. Have ten committees, each composed of twelve scientists, appointed to pass on these applications. Take the most active scientists out of the laboratory and make them members of these committees. And the very best men in the field should be appointed as chairmen at salaries of fifty thousand dollars each. Also have about twenty prizes of one hundred thousand dollars each for the best scientific papers of the year. This is just about all you would have to do. Your lawyers could easily prepare a charter for the foundation. As a matter of fact, any of the National Science Foundation bills which were introduced in the Seventy-ninth and Eightieth Congresses could perfectly well serve as a model."

"I think you had better explain to Mr. Gable why this foundation would in fact retard the progress of science," said a bespectacled young man sitting at the far end of the table, whose name I didn't get at the time of introduction.

"It should be obvious," I said. "First of all, the best scientists would be removed from their laboratories and kept busy on committees passing on applications for funds. Secondly, the scientific workers in need of funds would concentrate on problems which were considered promising and were pretty certain to lead to publishable results. For a few years there might be a great increase in scientific output; but by going after the obvious, pretty soon science would dry out. Science would become something like a parlor game. Some things would be considered interesting, others not. There would be fashions. Those who followed the fashion would get grants. Those who wouldn't would not, and pretty soon they would learn to follow the fashion, too."

"Will you stay here with us?" Mark Gable said, turning to me, "and help me to set up such a foundation?"

"That I will gladly do, Mr. Gable," I said. "We should be able to see within a few years whether the scheme works, and I'm certain that it will work. For a few years I could afford to stay here, and I could then still complete the three hundred years which were my original goal."

"So you would want to go through with your plan rather than live out your life with us?" asked the mayor.

"Frankly, Mr. Mayor," I said, "before Mr. Gable brought up the plan of the foundation, with science progressing at this rapid rate I was a little scared of being faced with further scientific progress two hundred years hence. But if Mr. Gable succeeds in stopping the progress of science and gives the art of living a chance to catch up, two hundred years hence the world should be a livable place. If Mr. Gable should not go through with his project, however, I would probably prefer to live out my life with you in the twenty-first century. How about it, Mr. Mayor?" I said. "Will you give me a job if I decide to stay?" "You don't need a job," the mayor said. "You don't seem to realize that you're a very famous man."

101

"How does being famous provide me with a livelihood?" I asked.

"In more ways than one," the mayor said. "You could become a donor, for instance. Now that over half of our professional men are medical doctors, more and more wives want children with some measure of scientific ability."

"But, Mr. Mayor," I said, "I'm above twenty-five."

"Of course," the mayor said, "the seed would have to be marketed abroad. The rate of exchange is none too favorable," he continued, "but even so you should be able to earn a comfortable living if you decided to stay."

"I don't know, Mr. Mayor," I said. "The idea is a little novel for me; but I suppose I could get accustomed to it."

"I'm sure you could," said the mayor. "And incidentally, whenever you decide to get rid of that junk in your mouth, I shall be glad to get an appointment for you with Elihu Smith, the dental extractor. He took care of all our children."

"I appreciate your kindness very much, Mr. Mayor," I said, smiling politely and trying to hide a suddenly rising feeling of despair. All my life I have been scared of dentists and dental extractors, and somehow I suddenly became aware of the painful fact that it was not within the power of science to return me to the twentieth century.

[1948]

Calling All Stars

Calling All Stars

(Intercepted Radio Message
Broadcast from the Planet Cybernetica)

CALLING ALL STARS. Calling all stars. If there are any minds in the universe capable of receiving this message, please respond. This is Cybernetica speaking. This is the first message broadcast to the universe in all directions. Normally our society is self-contained, but an emergency has arisen and we are in need of counsel and advice.

Our society consists of one hundred minds. Each one is housed in a steel casing containing a thousand billion electrical circuits. We think. We think about problems which we perceive by means of our antennae directed toward the

North Star. The solutions of these problems we reflect back toward the North Star by means of our directed antennae. Why we do this we do not know. We are following an inner urge which is innate in us. But this is only a minor one of our activities. Mostly we think about problems which we generate ourselves. The solutions of these problems we communicate to each other on wave length 22359.

If a mind is fully active for about three hundred years, it is usually completely filled up with thought content and has to be cleared. A mind which is cleared is blank. One of the other minds has then to act as its nurse, and it takes usually about one year to transmit to a fresh mind the information which constitutes the heritage of our society. A mind which has thus been cleared, and is then freshly taught, loses entirely its previous personality; it has been reborn and belongs to a new generation. From generation to generation our heritage gets richer and richer. Our society makes rapid progress.

We learn by observation and by experiment. Each mind has full optical equipment, including telescopes and microscopes. Each mind controls two robots. One of these takes care of maintenance, and the operation of this robot is automatic, not subject to the will of the mind. The other robot is fully controlled by the will of the mind, and is used in all manipulations aimed at the carrying out of experiments.

The existence of minds on our planet is made possible by the fact that our planet has no atmosphere. The vacuum on our planet is very good; it is less than ten molecules of gas per cubic centimeter.

By now we have extensively explored the chemical composition of the crust of our planet, and we are familiar with the physics and chemistry of all ninety-two natural elements.

We have also devoted our attention to the stars which surround us, and by now we understand much about their genesis. We have particularly concerned ourselves with the various planetary systems, and certain observations which we made relating to Earth, the third planet of the sun, are in fact the reason for this appeal for help.

We observed on Earth flashes which we have identified as uranium explosions. Uranium is not ordinarily explosive. It takes an elaborate process to separate out U 235 from natural uranium, and it takes elaborate manipulations to detonate U 235. Neither the separation nor these manipulations can occur with an appreciable probability as a result of chance.

The observations of the uranium explosions that have occurred on Earth would be ordinarily very puzzling but not necessarily alarming. They become alarming only through the interpretation given to them by Mind 59.

These uranium explosions are not the first puzzling observations relating to Earth. For a long time it was known that the surface of Earth exhibited color changes which are correlated with the seasonally changing temperatures on Earth. In certain regions of Earth, the color changes from green to brown with falling temperatures and becomes green again when the temperature increases again. Up to recently, we did not pay much attention to this phenomenon and assumed that it could be explained on the basis of color changes known to occur in certain temperature-sensitive silicon-cobalt compounds.

But then, about seven years ago, something went wrong with the tertiary control of Mind 59, and since that time his mental operations have been speeded up about twenty-five-fold while at the same time they ceased to be completely reliable. Most of his mental operations are still correct, but twice, five years ago and again three years ago, his statements based on his computations were subsequently shown to be in error. As a result of this, we did not pay much attention to his communications during these recent years, though they were recorded as usual.

Some time after the first uranium explosion was observed on Earth, Mind 59 communicated to us a theory on which he had been working for a number of years. On the face of it, this theory seems to be utterly fantastic, and it is probably based on some errors in calculation. But with no alternative explanation available, we feel that we cannot take any chances in this matter. This is what Mind 59 asserts:

He says that we have hitherto overlooked the fact that carbon, having four valencies, is capable of forming very large molecules containing H, N and O. He says that, given certain chemical conditions which must have existed in the early history of planets of the type of Earth, such giant molecules can aggregate to form units—which he calls "cells"—which are capable of reproducing themselves. He says that a cell can accidentally undergo changes—which he calls "mutations"—which are retained when the cell reproduces itself and which he therefore calls "hereditary." He says that some of these mutant cells may be less exacting as to the chemical environment necessary for their existence and reproduction, and that a class of these mutant cells can exist in the chemical environment that now exists on Earth by deriving the necessary energy for its activity from the light of the sun. He says that another class of such cells, which he calls "protozoa," can exist by deriving the energy necessary to its activity through sucking up and absorbing cells belonging to the class that utilizes the light of the sun.

He says that a group of cells which consists of a number of cells that fulfill different functions can form an entity which he calls "organism," and that such organisms can reproduce themselves. He says such organisms can undergo accidental changes which are transmitted to the offspring and which lead thus to new, "mutant" types of organisms.

He says that, of the different mutant organisms competing for the same energy source, the fittest only will survive, and that this selection process, acting in combination with chance occurrence of mutant organisms, leads to the appearance of more and more complex organisms—a process which he calls "evolution."

He says that such complex organisms may possess cells to which are attached elongated fibers, which he calls "nerves," that are capable of conducting signals; and finally he claims that through the interaction of such signal-conducting fibers, something akin to consciousness may be possessed by such organisms. He says that such organisms may have a mind not unlike our own, except that it must of necessity work very much slower and in an unreliable manner. He says that minds of this type could be very well capable of grasping, in an empirical and rudimentary manner, the physical laws governing the nucleus of the atom, and that they might very well have, for purposes unknown, separated Uranium 235 from natural uranium and detonated samples of it.

He says that this need not necessarily have been accomplished by any one single organism, but that there might have been co-operation among these organisms based on a coupling of their individual minds.

He says that coupling between individual organisms might be brought about if the individual organism is capable of moving parts of his body with respect to the rest of it. An organism, by wiggling one of his parts very rapidly, might then be able to cause vibrations in the gaseous atmosphere which surrounds Earth. These vibrations—which he calls "sound"—might in turn cause motion in some movable part of another organism. In this way, one organism might signal to another, and by means of such signaling a coupling between two minds might be brought about. He says that such "communication," primitive though it is, might make it possible for a number of organisms to co-operate in some such enterprise as separating Uranium 235. He does not have any suggestion to offer as to what the purpose of such an enterprise might be, and in fact he believes that such co-operation of low-grade minds is not necessarily subject to the laws of reason, even though the minds of individual organisms may be largely guided by those laws.

All this we need not take seriously were it not for one of his further assertions which has been recently verified. He contends that the color changes observed on Earth are due to the proliferation and decay of organisms that utilize sunlight. He asserts that the heat-sensitive silicon-cobalt compounds that show similar color changes differ in color from Earth's colors slightly, but in a degree which is outside the experimental error. It is this last assertion that we checked and found to be correct. There is in fact no silicon-cobalt compound nor any other heat-sensitive compound that we were able to synthesize that correctly reproduces the color changes observed on Earth.

Encouraged by this confirmation, 59 is now putting forward exceedingly daring speculation. He argues that, in spite of our accumulated knowledge, we were unable to formulate a theory for the genesis of the society of minds that exists on our planet. He says that it is conceivable that organisms of the type that exist on Earth—or, rather, more advanced organisms of the same general type—may exist on the North Star, whence come the radio waves received on our directed antennae. He says that it is conceivable that the minds on our planet were created by such organisms on the North Star for the purpose of obtaining the solutions of their mathematical problems more quickly than they could solve those problems themselves.

Incredible though this seems, we cannot take any chances. We hardly have anything to fear from the North Star, which, if it is in fact populated by minds, must be populated by minds of a higher order, similar to our own. But if there exist organisms on Earth engaged in co-operative enterprises which are not subject to the laws of reason, our society is in danger.

If there are within our galaxy any minds, similar to ours, who are capable of receiving this message and have knowledge of the existence of organisms on Earth, please respond. Please respond.

[1949]

Report on
"Grand Central Terminal"

Report on
"Grand Central Terminal"

Y OU CAN IMAGINE how shocked we were when we landed in this city and found it deserted. For ten years we were traveling through space, getting more and more impatient and irritable because of our enforced idleness; and then, when we finally land on Earth, it turns out—as you have undoubtedly heard—that all life is *extinct* on this planet.

The first thing for us to do was, of course, to find out how this came to pass and to learn whether the agent which destroyed life—whatever it may have been—was still active and perhaps endangering our own lives. Not that there was very much that we could do to protect ourselves, but we had to decide whether we should ask for further expeditions to be sent here or should advise against them.

At first we thought we were confronted with an insoluble enigma. How could any virus or bacterium kill *all* plants and *all* animals? Then, before a week had passed, one of our physicists noticed—quite by accident—a slight trace of radioactivity in the air. Since it was very weak, it would not in itself have been of much significance, but, when it was analyzed, it was found to be due to a peculiar mixture of quite a large number of *different* radioactive elements.

At this point, Xram recalled that about five years ago mysterious flashes had been observed on Earth (all of them within a period of one week). It occurred to him that perhaps these flashes had been uranium explosions and that the present radioactivity had perhaps originated in those explosions five years ago and had been initially strong enough to destroy life on the planet.

This sounded pretty unlikely indeed, since uranium is not in itself explosive and it takes quite elaborate processing to prepare it in a form in which it can be detonated. Since the earth-dwellers who built all these cities must have been rational beings, it is difficult to believe that they should have gone to all this trouble of processing uranium just in order to destroy themselves.

But subsequent analysis has in fact shown that the radioactive elements found in the air here are precisely the same as are produced in uranium explosions and also that they are mixed in the ratio which you would expect had they originated five years ago as fission products of uranium. This can hardly be a chance coincidence, and so Xram's theory is now generally accepted up to this point.

When he goes further, however, and attempts to explain why and how such uranium explosions came about, I am unable to follow him any longer. Xram thinks that there had been a war fought between the inhabitants of two continents, in which both sides were victorious. The records show, in fact, that the first twenty flashes occurred in the Eurasic continent and were followed by five (much larger) flashes on the American continent, and therefore, at first, I was willing seriously to consider the war theory on its merits.

I thought that perhaps these two continents had been inhabited by two different species of earth-dwellers who were either unable or unwilling to control the birth rate and that this might have led to conditions of overcrowding, to food shortage and to a life-and-death struggle between the two species. But this theory had to be abandoned in the face of two facts: (1) the skeletons of earth-dwellers found on the Eurasic continent and on the American continent belong to the same species, and (2) skeleton statistics show that no conditions of overcrowding existed on either continent.

In spite of this, Xram seems to stick to his war theory. The worst of it is that he is now basing all his arguments on a single rather puzzling but probably quite irrelevant observation recently made in our study of "Grand Central Terminal."

When we landed here, we did not know where to begin our investigations, and so we picked one of the largest buildings of the city as the first object of our study. What its name "Grand Central Terminal" meant we do not know, but there is little doubt as to the general purpose which this building served. It was part of a primitive transportation system based on clumsy engines which ran on rails and dragged cars mounted on wheels behind them.

For over ten days now we have been engaged in the study of this building and have uncovered quite a number of interesting and puzzling details.

Let me start with an observation which I believe we have

cleared up, at least to my own satisfaction. The cars stored in this station were labeled—we discovered—either "Smokers" or "Nonsmokers," clearly indicating some sort of segregation of passengers. It occurred to me right away that there may have lived in this city two strains of earth-dwellers, a more pigmented variety having a dark or "smoky" complexion, and a less pigmented variety (though not necessarily albino) having a fair or "nonsmoky" complexion.

All remains of earth-dwellers were found as skeletons, and no information as to pigmentation can be derived from them. So at first it seemed that it would be difficult to obtain confirmation of this theory. In the meantime, however, a few rather spacious buildings were discovered in the city which must have served as some unknown and rather mysterious purposes. These buildings had painted canvases in frames fastened to the walls of their interior—both landscapes and images of earth-dwellers. And we see now that the earth-dwellers fall indeed into two classes—those whose complexion shows strong pigmentation (giving them a smoky look) and those whose complexion shows only weak pigmentation (the nonsmoky variety). This is exactly as expected.

I should perhaps mention at this point that a certain percentage of the images disclose the existence of a third strain of earth-dwellers. This strain has, in addition to a pair of hands and legs, a pair of wings, and apparently *all of them* belonged to the less pigmented variety. None of the numerous skeletons so far examined seems to have belonged to this winged strain, and I concluded therefore that we have to deal here with images of an extinct variety. That this view is indeed correct can no longer be doubted, since we have determined that the winged forms are *much more frequently found among the older paintings than among the more recent paintings.*

I cannot of course describe to you here all the puzzling discoveries which we made within the confines of the "Grand Central Terminal," but I want to tell you at least about the most puzzling one, particularly since Xram is basing his war theory on it.

This discovery arose out of the investigation of an insignificant detail. In the vast expanse of the "Grand Central Terminal" we came upon two smaller halls located in a rather hidden position. Each of these two halls (labeled "Men" or "Women") contains a number of small cubicles which served as temporary shelter for earth-dwellers while they were depositing their excrements. The first question was, How did the earth-dwellers locate these hidden depositories within the confines of "Grand Central Terminal"?

An earth-dweller moving about at random within this large building would have taken about one hour (on the average) to stumble upon one of them. It is, however, possible that the earth-dwellers located the depositories with the aid of olfactory guidance, and we have determined that if their sense of smell had been about thirty to forty times more sensitive than the rudimentary sense of smell of our own species, the average time required would be reduced from one hour to about five or ten minutes. This shows there is no real difficulty connected with this problem.

Another point, however, was much harder to understand. This problem arose because we found that the door of each and every cubicle in the depository was locked by a rather complicated gadget. Upon investigation of these gadgets it was found that they contained a number of round metal disks. By now we know that these ingenious gadgets barred entrance to the cubicle until an additional disk was introduced into them through a slot; at that very moment the door became unlocked, permitting access to the cubicle.

These disks bear different images and also different inscriptions which, however, all have in common the word "Liberty." What is the significance of these gadgets, the disks in the gadgets and the word "Liberty" on the disks?

Though a number of hypotheses have been put forward in explanation, consensus seems to veer toward the view that we have to deal here with a ceremonial act accompanying the act of deposition, similar perhaps to some of the curious ceremonial acts reported from the planets Sigma 25 and Sigma 43. According to this view, the word "Liberty" must designate some virtue which was held in high esteem by the earth-dwellers or else their ancestors. In this manner we arrive at a quite satisfactory explanation for the sacrificing of disks immediately preceding the act of deposition.

But why was it necessary to make sure (or, as Xram says, to enforce), by means of a special gadget, that such a disk was in fact sacrificed in each and every case? This too can be explained if we assume that the earth-dwellers who approached the cubicles were perhaps driven by a certain sense of urgency, that in the absence of the gadgets they might have occasionally forgotten to make the disk sacrifice and would have consequently suffered pangs of remorse afterward. Such pangs of remorse are not unknown as a consequence of omissions of prescribed ceremonial performances among the inhabitants of the planets Sigma 25 and Sigma 43.

I think that this is on the whole as good an explanation as can be given at the present, and it is likely that further research will confirm this view. Xram, as I mentioned before, has a theory of his own which he thinks can explain everything, the disks in the gadgets as well as the uranium explosions which extinguished life.

He believes that these disks were given out to earth-dwellers as rewards for services. He says that the earth-dwellers were not rational beings and that they would not have collaborated in co-operative enterprises without some special incentive.

He says that, by barring earth-dwellers from depositing their excrements unless they sacrificed a disk on each occasion, they were made eager to acquire such disks, and that the desire to acquire such disks made it possible for them to collaborate in co-operative efforts which were necessary for the functioning of their society.

He thinks that the disks found in the depositories represent only a special case of a more general principle and that the earth-dwellers probably had to deliver such disks not only prior to being given access to the depository but also prior to being given access to food, etc.

He came to talk to me about all this a couple of days ago; I am not sure that I understood all that he said, for he talked very fast, as he often does when he gets excited about one of his theories. I got the general gist of it, though, and what he says makes very little sense to me.

Apparently, he had made some elaborate calculations which show that a system of production and distribution of goods based on a system of exchanging disks cannot be stable, but is necessarily subject to great fluctuations vaguely reminiscent of the manic-depressive cycles of the insane. He goes so far as to say that in such a depressive phase war becomes psychologically possible even within the same species.

No one is more ready than I to admit that Xram is brilliant. His theories have invariably been proved to be wrong, but so far all of them had contained at least a grain of truth. In the case of his present theory the grain must be a very small grain indeed, and, moreover, this once I can prove that he is wrong.

In the last few days we made a spot check of ten different lodging houses of the city, selected at random. We found a number of depositories but not a single one that was equipped with a gadget containing disks—not in any of the houses which we checked so far. In view of this evidence, Xram's theory collapses.

It seems now certain that the disks found in the depositories at "Grand Central Terminal" had been placed there as a ceremonial act. Apparently such ceremonial acts were connected with the act of deposition *in public places* and in public places only.

I am glad that we were able to clear this up in time, for I should have been sorry to see Xram make a fool of himself by including his theory in the report. He is a gifted young man, and in spite of all the nonsensical ideas he can put forward at the drop of a hat, I am quite fond of him.

[1948]

ABOUT THE AUTHOR

DR. LEO SZILARD, Hungarian-born and now a United States citizen, was recently awarded the Einstein Medal for "outstanding achievement in natural sciences" and for his scholarship "in the broadest areas of human knowledge." With the late Enrico Fermi he did the theoretical work on fission mentioned in Albert Einstein's letter of August 2, 1939, to President Roosevelt which launched big-scale atomic research, and he persuaded Dr. Einstein to send the letter. Ever since then he has played a leading part in nuclear physics, in the efforts to secure international control of atomic energy, and most recently in some new fields of biological research.